THE
BANDIT'S OF
BANDARSON

THE BANDIT'S OF BANDARSON

M. W. KOHLER

iUniverse LLC
Bloomington

THE BANDIT'S OF BANDARSON

iUniverse books may be ordered through booksellers or by contacting:

iUniverse LLC
1663 Liberty Drive
Bloomington, IN 47403
www.iuniverse.com
1-800-Authors (1-800-288-4677)

ISBN: 978-1-4917-2468-2 (sc)
ISBN: 978-1-4917-2469-9 (e)

Library of Congress Control Number: 2014902512

Printed in the United States of America.

iUniverse rev. date: 02/10/2014

NOTES FROM THE AUTHOR

This is the fifth book of *The Valley* series. Years had passed since the Dark War, and the lives of those of all domains had found peace. Even Zentler had found a contentment within their world. Then the Fates decided that contentment, should not be, and a night came that destroyed the peace and happiness, of all of Zentler. Fear again came to those of magic. When Glornina received a message from Cartope, all knew that a new threat had come, different than those known before.

Prologue

Years before the Dark War had been fought, in the highly protected, well hidden domain of Bandarson, in the gloomy castle that was in the center of the capital city, Brandaro, the new Ruler for only a year now, sprawled on the resplendent couch, that was called his throne. The two beautiful, young women, who shared his cruel pleasures, sat nearby, talking of what he had done, and they were laughing. He thought of the pleasures he had found in the horrible torture of the man, and the violent raping of the woman. He was also becoming consumed by what the screaming man had told him, and the terrified confirmation of that information from the woman, before he had satisfied his perverted pleasures, with the taking of her.

For many years now, he had been hearing the stories from the raiding parties commanders, that they had heard of what they said was called, Rightful Magic. They had also reported that it was thought that there were two domains, the Realm, and the Plain, that were the strongest in this magic. He had at first, only dreamed of the taking of them, and the wealth they were sure to contain. Later, he began to feel a new desire. The desire for the power he could gain, from the magic of these two places. The intensity of his desire grew stronger, and stronger, but he was constantly frustrated that he could never learn where these domains were to be found. Then, the two were brought to him, and he had finally learned the location of the planet that held the Plain. From those of the Plain, he would learn the location of the Realm.

But, his thoughts could not long be deferred from the disturbing realization that the supply of magic enhancing amulets, his father had left him, was getting quite low. He knew he had to return to the domain that he and his father, had first raided. The gains of that raid had led to the establishing of Bandarson. He knew he had to get more of the amulets, to be able to conquer this Plain! The years began to pass, as he plotted his assaults.

Chapter One

Gordon needed to squint as he stepped from the shadow of the interior of City Hall, onto the large porch, and into the bright, late Saturday afternoon sunshine. He smiled, as he stopped at the top of the wide steps. He casually pulled a cigar case from the inside pocket of his suit coat, and pulled one from the case, as his eyes slowly caressed the view before him. As he returned the case to his inside pocket, he reached into the side pocket of his coat, pulling the clipper. He clipped the end of the cigar, and placed the clipped end between his front teeth. He returned the clipper to his coat pocket, as he pulled a match from his vest pocket. Using just the nail of his right thumb, he lit the match, and casually lit the end of the cigar. He tossed the match into one of the two receptors that had been placed at the top of the stairs, for such things. He pushed the side of his coat back and put his left hand into his pants pocket. He slowly turned the cigar, still held by his lips, with his right hand, as he continued to look around the town of Zentler. He just had to smile. "Another beautiful spring day," he said softly to himself, around the cigar.

"Good night, Mr. Mayor," young Penelopy Barns said, as she passed him and went down the steps. Gordon looked to the girl, who was a part time filing clerk, and nodded. *Well formed*, he thought, but didn't dare say, for he was sure that somehow, her mother would find out, and make his life, a hell. The fact that there were very few, if any, in the town of Zentler, especially himself, who liked her mother, in any way, flashed through his mind.

"Good night, Penelopy," he called after her. "See you Monday," he added. She reached the bottom of the steps, and turned slightly. She smiled, nodded, waved, and then continued on to the home she shared with her widowed, rich, egocentric, mother. He stood at the top of the steps, his feet spaced wide, looking over his town, as he puffed slowly on the cigar, that was held by his lips and right hand. He was pleased with the progress the town had made, to become what it was. He remembered the town of his youth, and the mayor, his grandfather, whom everyone had simply called, Willy. The man had guided Zentler to be a leading example for many towns, on what had become known as Zentler Road.

He had been elected mayor shortly after Willy had passed on, and he was very proud of the innovations he had brought to Zentler. The naming of all of the streets of the town, and the cobble stone paving that had been done, he had initiated as soon as he had become mayor. He was especially proud of the new gas street lights that had been placed just a year ago. He smiled as he thought that this town was now a town of advancement, and safety. There was little, or no crime here, simply because there was no need of it. As he started down the steps, he thought that a beer would taste just right. He walked across the exceedingly large lawn that fronted the Court House, across Main Street, down several doors, and into the most popular of the three taverns in Zentler, simply called, "Pete's". He was warmly welcomed, for Gordon was well liked in Zentler.

"Xanaporia know you're here, Mr. Mayor?" Pete asked, louder than was needed, with a teasing tone in his voice, as he set a mug full of beer in front of him. Gordon saw that Pete had that funny, lopsided grin on his face, he always used when he thought he was making a funny comment. Gordon frowned at him, as the tavern owner turned, and went back to the chess game he was playing with old Danner, at the end of the bar.

"Her and the kids are visiting her aunt," Gordon told Pete's back. "Besides, I do not need her permission to have a beer," he told the room in general. Gordon heard the badly hidden chuckles from several of the tables. He knew that most all of the town knew of the amount that he used to drink, and his wife's' displeasure, when he did now. He didn't want to think of what Xanaporia was going to say, when she got back from her visit to the Plain.

The usual tavern banter broke out, and the Chief of Police, who had just gotten off work himself, suckered Gordon into a game of darts. Beers, and other beverages, continued to be drunk, and time passed. At first, no one even turned as the door opened, but very quickly, a silence settled over the tavern, as more, and more, looked at the one standing just inside the doorway. Gordon and the Chief, who were in heated debate about the point value of a thrown dart by Gordon, were the last to turn, and they both wished they hadn't.

"Who b'long dis?" asked the coarse graveled voice, of the fattest, tall, man, any had ever seen, as he held the one deputy of Zentler, dangling from his huge fist, with a very frightened look on his face. The fat man then threw the Deputy to the floor.

"Now see here," the Chief said, as he stepped forward, his uniform clearly designating his authority. "What do you think you're doing?" The fat man's smile grew as he took a large step forward himself, and two more, almost the size of the fat man, stepped in, behind him. The Chief stopped, his eyes growing wider, with the appearance of the other two. The fat man laughed.

"Any tings I's wans," the fat man said, and laughed louder. He then pointed a fat finger at Pete, standing behind the bar, quite wide eyed. "I's wans sump'n ta drink, now!" he told the frightened Pete. Pete nodded rapidly, and put a bottle on the bar. The fat man looked at it, and then to Pete. "Ya's dosn't tinks I's got me's manners? Gi me's a mugs!" Pete again nodded quickly, and put a mug next to the bottle. The fat man looked at him, and his eyes narrowed. "Pour!" he roared. Pete grabbed the bottle, and turned it up, over the mug. He was shaking so much that not all that came from the bottle, went into the mug. When Pete righted the bottle, and pushed the mug towards the fat man, the fat man grabbed it, and drained it. He smacked his lips, and nodded. "Mor's," he told Pete, slamming the mug on the bar; "and me mates," he added, jerking his fat thumb over his shoulder. The two with him nodded with grins that showed their horrible teeth to all. Pete put two more mugs on the bar, and tried to fill them. The fat man's smiled grew even wider as he watched the deputy, crawl past the chief, and under a table near the back of the room.

"Chief, do something," Gordon said turning to him. The Chief of Police, looked to him in anger.

"What, and how?" he asked none to calmly, or quietly. It was then that the sounds of breaking glass, busting wood, screams, and yells, were heard drifting passed the three in the doorway. The fat man grinned at the chief, and lifted one brow.

"Me's and me's mates, gonna ta see whacha's got in dis town," he told the Chief. "Ya's dosn't mind dos ya?" He started to laugh, never taking his menacing eyes from the Chief, as the chief just stared angrily back at him. There came a voice from behind the fat man.

"Capt'n, dey's ain't got hardly nottin here!" the voice called. The fat man just shook his head sadly, still looking into the Chiefs eyes. He then looked the one to his left, and gave a short nod. That big man went behind the bar. He grabbed several bottles, and passed them to the other silent one. He then started to break everything. Bottles, mirror, anything he could get his hands on. Pete tried to rush him and stop the destruction of his tavern, but the much bigger man simply backhanded him, knocking him down, and out. The breaking bottles of brandy, and whiskey, splashed the liquors all over the bar, and around it. The man then came out from behind the bar, took one of the bottles he had previously passed to his cohort, and they went out the door. The fat man smiled as he pulled a match from his vest pocket. He looked at it as he slowly turned it with his fingers. He then casually struck it on one of the few dry spots on the bar, and looked to the chief, smiling.

"Should'a had mor's," he said calmly, and tossed the match at the bar. The liquor flared up, driving all the patrons towards the rear of the building. The fat man turned around, and walked out. He stopped just outside, and looked around. "Burn it all!" he yelled, as he walked away. Someone snuck under the end of the bar, and pulled Pete out of the nearing flames. The patrons all ran for the back door, as the wood building quickly caught, and started to burn. Gordon, one of the two men now carrying Pete, suddenly remembered seeing the amulet the fat man had wore around his fat neck, and he could have sworn, it looked just like an Amplifying Stone!

———

"It's going to be a beautiful night," Mentalon, grandson of Tommy, and easily as strong a sensitive as his grandfather, told his wife, Xanadera, as they sat down on the porch of the house his Great, Great, Grandparents, Bill and Kathy Zentler, had built. She nodded, with a small smile, and sipped on the glass of wine she held.

Mentalon suddenly tensed, as the seeing of the events unfolding in Zentler, came to him. When the seeing ended, he stood, and without a word to Xanadera, went into the house. He could feel Xanadera's closeness, as she followed him. Mentalon contacted Quansloe, the Keeper of the Plain, on his orb.

Quansloe, at first, did not want to believe what he was being told. "Are you serious?" he asked Mentalon.

"You have to investigate this," his wife Hannah, said, rather loudly, placing her hand on his arm.

"Quansloe," Xanaporia, Gordon's wife said, and all could hear the fear for her husband's safety, in her voice. Quansloe could see the nodding heads of Xanaporia's two children, as well as their mates.

"I am completely serious," Mentalon said from the ob.

"Quansloe?" Hannah whispered. Quansloe looked from the orb, then to those gathered around him, and nodded. He turned back to the orb.

"Keep me informed of anything else you might see." Mentalon nodded, and broke the connection. He turned back the others'. "Let's get Cory and Felicia from the Valley, and see what is happening," he told them, and they all headed for the permanent portal to the Valley, at a run.

Cory, the now Caretaker of the Valley, was leading as the horses cleared the trees, well east of Zentler. The burning town they all saw, made them rein in the horses. "Oh God!" Xanaporia screamed, and heeled her horse to a full gallop. The rest followed immediately, still nodding their agreed shock. Just outside of the burning town, they drew their horses up. Barttel, Xanaporia's son, gathered reins, as the rest ran for the town.

"Don't let anyone see your magic!" Quansloe yelled to them all, as they entered the town of Zentler.

We have to find Gordon!" Xanaporia yelled to all. She was the first to find her husband, and she tried not to cry as she held him.

"We must tell the Overseer of these murderers," Gordon told Quansloe angrily, after he had found Quansloe and had told the Keeper what he knew. Quansloe nodded.

"Let's take care of the people first. We can tell the Overseer in the morning," Quansloe told him. The obviously very shaken, and very angry, Gordon, with Xanaporia, and their children, and their wife and husband, nodded, and did what they could for the survivors of the attack.

"What's the total?" Quansloe asked Gordon, when the Mayor joined him at the west side of the destroyed town. The mornings sun causing them to shade their eyes, as they walked east through the town.

"The bastards have taken jewels, gold, and silver, in any form they could find it," Gordon growled. "They've taken the finest of cloths from the McFurgal store, as well as anything else that was of value, including most of the food stock. They even took the two golden figurines of Christ, from the church!" Gordon's voice clearly showed his shock. His voice went deeper, and his anger became greater with his next words; "They also took nine young women!" Quansloe stopped, and looked to the enraged Mayor, his eyes wide. Gordon's head nodded back to him, but it was his rage was what was staring into the Keepers eyes. Quansloe looked around the almost completely destroyed town. He saw the makeshift structure that had been built, and that some the women of the town, were now trying to cook a breakfast for the exhausted, and still in shock residents. He glanced at the Mayor, who was seeing the same things. He turned, and they continued east, through the town, in silence. When they reached the far eastern end of the town, they both turned back, seeing the unbelievable destruction that had been done.

"It is time the Overseer was told," Quansloe said. Gordon nodded. They stepped from the sight of witnesses, and disappeared.

⟶•◦❈◦◗❈◖◦❈◦•⟵

Quansloe and Gordon appeared in the entrance hall of the palace, and Namson, Glornina, Zachia, Namson and Glornina's oldest, and Drandysee, Elder of the Guardians, were waiting for them.

"How bad is it?" Namson asked, as soon as they had arrived. Gordon looked furious.

"Most all of the businesses are burned to the ground, as well as some fifteen to twenty homes, completely gone. Another twenty or thirty were damaged severely by fire. Another fifteen, or so, not so bad. The rest are alright, as these bastards had mostly stayed to the center of town. There are over twenty dead, over thirty seriously wounded, and around fifty, with minor injuries," he told the Overseer of the Realm, and then frowned even more. "There are nine young women missing, thought to be kidnapped!" Glornina gasped, her eyes wide, as she looked to Gordon.

"Gordon has something else to say Namson, and I think you need to hear it," Quansloe said and they all looked to the mayor. Gordon looked to the Overseer. His angry eyes, also held a look of worry.

"It looked like the fat man, the one we assume was the leader, because he had been called Capt'n, was wearing an amulet around his neck, and it looked like a Amplifying Stone!" he said quietly, calmly, and fiercely. Silence followed his words.

"I sent out bats to see if they could find the band," Quansloe stated; "but they came back, and said that they could not find any sign the band had traveled very far. Just outside of town actually. A group that size had to have left some sort of trail, but the bats found nothing. It was as though they had just simply vanished," Quansloe added.

"Robbers, with magical powers?" Glornina asked in a worried whisper, looking to her husband.

"Robbers, kidnappers, and murderers," Gordon growled. "Three of those dead, were but children!" Glornina gasped again, her hand going to her mouth, and looked down, fighting her tears.

"Let's go to my office," Namson said quietly, and turned. Taking Glornina's arm, he led them all into his office, near the rear of the Palace. No one noticed the shadow that pulled back from the corner, on the balcony, and slipped down the hallway of the second floor.

—◦◦◦◦—

When they had all settled into chairs, and the couch, they looked to the thoughtful Overseer. "Drandysee," Namson said after a few minutes of thought; "find out from any of the lesser domains you can locate, especially the ones that are only partially magical, if there are any other reports of these robbers." The Elder of the Guardians nodded, and left. Namson turned to his son. "Ask Mentalon if he has had any sensing of these robbers, in any way."

"Mentalon was the one to alert me," Quansloe interrupted. Namson nodded, and returned his eyes to his son. "Checking with only the Keepers of Magic, contact Ventoria, Dolaris, Vistalin, Calisonnos, and Corsendora. Find out if any of the seers of their domains, have felt any sensing of these robbers, or know of any events they might have been involved in." Zachia nodded, and he left. Namson looked to Glornina, and she shook her head, once, with a small shrug. She had had no sensing of the robbers. Namson wondered why as he turned to Gordon. "Now I want you to tell me everything, from the beginning. What happened, as closely as you can remember, and then, what you found out later." Gordon nodded, and began his telling.

—

"Somora," Baldor sent his thoughts, from the large broom closet. "There was a raid on the town of Zentler, and they took much, including the kidnapping of nine young women." He waited for the reply of his King.

"That confirms what Delores sent, late last night," Somora said. "Keep your ears open, and let me know what the Overseer does about this."

"Yes, My Lord," Baldor answered, and eased from the closet.

—

As Pinsikar hurried from the meeting with one of his spies, he passed one of the richer bandits mansions. He suddenly heard the angry roaring of that bandit, and the answering shriek of a dwarf. He averted his eyes from the sound, and frowned, for he could remember the time that he had spent in the servitude of a bandit, before Brandaro had rescued him. He had been very young when he first went to work for the bandit. He had been taught the tricks of being a spy, from that bandit. He had also learned that most humans could not, and would not, ever respect dwarves, ever. He growled quietly, with the memories of the cruelties that had been done, to teach him his place in the society of Bandarson. He realized that although he was a normal height for a male dwarf, at four and a half foot tall, he was to be constantly tormented, by all humans, for his height. He sniffled, once, and then rubbed the end of his long, hooked nose, as he walked towards the dismal castle of the Ruler of all Bandarson. He wiped his finger on his breeches, and then ran his hand over the sparse hair that grew on his head, flattening his rearward pointing ears as he did. He chuckled as he remembered his reward for the first successful spying he had done. He remembered the naked, young, female that had been brought into the room, where his master had congratulated him. He had seen many female dwarves before, and he had felt the urge to have one, but his master had never allowed it. His eyes covered her body, from head to toe. He saw that she was actually taller than he, by at least six inches, which he had seen with all female dwarves, and had much more hair on her head than he did.

"Go ahead," his master had said, grinning a horrible grin. "Take her." He hesitated, realizing that he was to have her, as all in the room watched. "Take her!" the bandit roared at him. He saw the fear in her eyes as he approached her. She had been trying to cover herself with her hands, and he began to feel a powerful excitement, as he began to take his clothes off. Although he could hear the laughter of the humans, he didn't think of them, as he took her. She cried and whined as he did it, and his excitement grew stronger. He stood, when he had finished, and looked to his master.

"Can I have her, as mine?" he had asked. His master had nodded, as he laughed. Pinsikar had gathered his clothes, pulled her from the floor, and took her to his quarters. He served that bandit for two more years, until Brandaro heard of his talents, as a spy, and he had come to Rulers service. He had brought the female with him.

Brandaro stared at the ugly creature that had been brought to his throne room. "What do you want?" he growled at it, for he had only just finished his breakfast, and he didn't like dealing with his duties until he had had a chance to adjust to the morning.

Lord Brandaro," the creature said with a deep bow. "My name is Garsalar, and I have come here to ask your aid, in the conquering of the Weretorians, who share our domain."

"Why would I be interested in helping your race?" Brandaro asked, beginning to feel anger for the creature. Garsalar looked to the Ruler, nervously.

"We Gargoyles, are like you Lord Brandaro. We need to rule our entire domain, and then to spread out, conquering others', to gain from their loss," The creature actually smiled as he spoke. Brandaro became enraged at the arrogance of it. He rose and charged the creature so quickly, it barely had time to look surprised before Brandaro's hands grabbed it. Garsalar screamed out, with his surprise, and pain, as Brandaro picked him from his feet, and started for the court yard. As he neared the gate, the guards quickly opened them, and Brandaro easily threw the Gargoyle, quite some distance outside of the gate. The ruler looked to two of the large guards, and pointed to Garsalar, with a nod. The Gargoyle saw the horrible grins of the guards, as they started for him. He quickly formed a portal, fleeing the presence of his sure death.

—·w··o·o·oo·oo·oo·oo·w··—

It was after lunch time, and Pinsikar, hurried through the dim, and dirty passageway, lit only by the occasional torch. He quietly mumbled to himself, making sure he had all of his facts ready for his report to Brandaro, as he went. After several turns, he emerged from the passageway, the opening of which was hidden by a large faded and dirty tapestry, into the receiving hall, and then up the three steps that led to the door of his Rulers throne room. He was frightened, but then, he was always frightened of one thing, or another, especially when alone. That's why he always whined when he talked. Besides the fact that all dwarves had a natural whine to their voices. He reached the door to the throne room, and began to knock in his usual, rapid fire way.

"Go away, you little bastard!" Morselia yelled through the door. There was nothing but contempt in her voice.

"Wait," the deep baritone voice of Brandaro stated. "Do not take on airs Morselia. Not ever again." There was a anger, and a harsh tone of warning in his voice. "Enter Pinsikar," Brandaro ordered. The dwarf lifted the latch, and pushed open the huge door. Without actually thinking about it, Pinsikar knew that the door had to be huge, to allow Brandaro to pass through it, for Brandaro was huge. Almost eight feet tall, and very well muscled, he was the biggest man in Bandarson. Pinsikar trembled, just slightly, as he came into the room.

When Pinsikar entered, the first person he saw was the black-haired Caratelia, Brandaro's second woman. She was absolutely gorgeous. The thin, almost transparent gown she wore, clearly showed all of the peaks, and valleys, of her body, causing Pinsikar to want to drool with desire. The second one he saw was red-headed Morselia, Brandaro's first woman. The sight of her added fuel to his desire. Caratelia was smaller than Morselia, though not by much. Morselia, closer the height of Brandaro, and possessing a magnificent figure, was a sight unto herself. There was not a male, of any species on Bandarson, who did not lust for Morselia. "What is it Pinsikar?" Brandaro asked patiently, pulling Pinsikar's attention from the women.

"Porkligor has returned from his raid, and he is raging," Pinsikar stated in his whiny voice. "He didn't get so much, and what he got, is not so very valuable. The only thing that he got, that has any chance of value, was nine young females to sell as slaves. But, to say it simple, he ain't gonna get much for them. They are too small to be of much use," the dwarf told his master, with a chuckle. Brandaro smiled, nodding.

"Inform Telposar to bring that fat waste of time to me, and to make sure the captain is calm when he does so. Tell him to also bring these girls, I want to look them over," Brandaro told the dwarf, smiling. Pinsikar nodded rapidly, and left, pulling the huge door closed behind him.

"Why do you keep that little creep?" Morselia asked as she turned to Brandaro. She didn't even question his desire to look the girls over, for that was his right as Ruler. He got first pick of any living thing brought to Bandarson, that was to be sold as a slave.

"He reminds me of a over sized, hairless, tailless, rat!" Caratelia said as she rose from the couch, heading for their private chambers, to change for the presence of Porkligor. Morselia laughed as she followed her.

"That is a perfect description Caratelia, perfect," Morselia said.

"Alright!" Brandaro bellowed, causing both women to jump, and look to him with fear. "I have told you both before, but I will tell you again, for the last time." There was a deep, deadly tone in his voice. "Pinsikar can do things I need done, in a way that is a benefit for me, and as a results, both of you! Now get changed, and I do not want to hear anymore, about your opinions concerning

Pinsikar!" Both women nodded, and scurried for the bedroom.

Pinsikar knocked on Telposar's door, fearfully. He, as well as everyone else, knew of the pleasure the man received when he tore someone to pieces. Pinsikar truly feared coming here, for Telposar hated him. The door suddenly jerked open, and the big man, almost as big as Brandaro, and completely naked, stared down at Pinsikar.

"What do you want runt?' Telposar asked, threateningly. Pinsikar's voice trembled, as well as whined.

"Brandaro wants you to go, and bring Porkligor to him, and calm him before you arrive. He said that you are also to bring the females he captured," Pinsikar told him meekly. Telposar laughed loudly.

"Is that fat idiot back?" Pinsikar nodded, rapidly. "Alright, you've delivered your message, now, get out of my sight!" he roared at the dwarf, bending slightly, with a glare at the dwarf. Pinsikar ran off. Telposar chuckled as he shut the door, and went to dress. When he entered his bed chambers, where the large, but not fat, and not particularly pretty woman, stared at him from the bed.

"You really don't like that dwarf, do you?" she asked, with a smile. Telposar went to the bed, grabbed her hair with his right hand, and easily lifted her almost completely from the bed. She didn't try to reach for his hand, or even flinch from the pain she must have felt. In fact, she smiled at the only man she thought deserved her.

"Belidaria, he wouldn't even make a good appetizer," he hissed at her, and dropped her back to the bed. She laughed, and watched as he began to dress.

"Can I come with you?" she asked. "I would like very much, to see that fat bastard get a good beating." He grinned at her, nodding slightly. She returned the grin, threw the small amount of blankets from her naked body, and dressed.

Jardilan, grandson of Jarpon and Katie, and now the of Keeper of Magic, of Dolaris, waited in his office, for his son, Jarsolan. Jardilan felt that his son was ready to take his place as Keeper. He waited for him now, to tell him of the conversation he had just finished with Zachia. He was a little surprised when the entire family walked into the room.

"What is all this?" he asked with a slight·grin. "I only asked for Jarsolan."

"Yes father," Jarsolan said; "but Quentia had a dream last night, that at first, Barrett thought a simple nightmare. After we all talked with her about it this morning, Quentoria and I realized that she had had a seeing." Jardilan smiled gently, as he looked to his granddaughter, whose belly was just beginning to swell with hers and Barrett's second child.

"What did you see dear?" Jardilan asked her. She tried to smile.

"A very fat man, in a saloon or something, standing, and grinning, as another big man destroyed what was behind the counter. Then, the one breaking everything, left with another, and the fat man struck a match, setting fire to the building. The Mayor of Zentler, Gordon, was there too," she told him. Jardilan looked at her for a moment, and then around the room.

"Yesterday, just after the sun had set, a band of robbers, and murderers, attacked Zentler, and stole what they could, destroying most all of the town by fire. They also kidnapped nine young women," he told them all. There were frightened eyes looking back at him.

There is no doubt of this?" Margelia, Jardilan's wife asked, in a whisper. Jardilan shook his head, and then went to his orb, and called to Zachia, as shocked looks were exchanged by the others'. Nobody noticed the one listening at the door, that was not quite closed.

———

Quoslon, grandson of Marie, had returned to the North West Domain to be Keeper of Magic, at the urgings of his mother, Narisha, now looked between Edward, his son, whom he had just yesterday, given the control of the North West Domain. Carla, Edward's wife, Karrie, Edward and Carla's youngest, and Narmon, her husband, not believing what he had heard. He looked again to his granddaughter, Karrie, who had taken after her mother, Carla, and was a powerful seer and talker.

"Are you sure this is what you've seen?" he asked her, as Xanalenor, Quoslon's wife, came into the room. Karrie nodded, and Xanalenor confirmed it.

"I've just talked with Margelia in Dolaris. She told me that her granddaughter, Quentia, has had a connected seeing," she said quietly, as she stopped next to Quoslon.

"Now, tell me again, what did you see," he asked Karrie, who had her mother's arm around her shoulders. Karrie cleared her throat, as she crossed her arm across her chest, and placed her hand on Carla's, that was on her shoulder, and told of her seeing.

"It was night, and there was a very fat, ugly man, leading a very large group of men out of Zentler, and there were some girls struggling to get free. When they got to a darkened area, they all vanished," she told him in a flat voice. Quoslon looked to Xanalenor.

"Quentia saw the same thing?" he asked. She shook her head.

"She saw the fat man, set a tavern in Zentler on fire, and she saw Gordon in the tavern at the time." Quoslon fought his grin.

"I bet Xanaporia mentioned that to him," he said quietly, thinking of his older sisters temper, and then his eyes opened wide as he looked to his wife. Again, she shook her head, placing her hand on his arm.

"She and the children were in the Plain when it happened," she told him calmly. Quoslon sighed and looked to the others.

"We better tell Zachia. He talked to me earlier, asking if anyone had had a seeing of what had happened in Zentler, and, it would seem there has been a couple anyway," he said, going to the orb, calling to Zachia. The silent individual, pretending to dust, listened to Quoslon's report from outside the room, and smiled.

———

Cartope, daughter of Castope, the ruler of Dark Magic, who had been killed in the war that the Realm had waged against her mother, was sitting in the lounger, relaxing, with her eyes closed, in the shade of the rather short, wide spread tree. Her mind wandered, and she remembered when she had first realize the love Ralsanac felt for her. It had taken her at least another month for her to deal with the fact that although older than she, he was actually her nephew. What had troubled her the most, then, was the fact that she found that she had feelings for him as well. She smiled as she remembered how the mental debate of what she was going to do about the situation, had been settled one morning, as she had bathed in the lake near the city they had built, mostly in the trees.

She had been shoulder deep in the warm water, and had just finished rinsing her hair. She wrung it as she waded towards the shore. She had reached about waist deep when she had seen that Ralsanac waited for her on the beach, holding a towel stretched out in his hands. A sudden wave of modesty had overcome her. She dropped into the water until she was covered to her neck.

"What are you doing there Ralsanac?" She had tried to make her question sound condemning, but it came out as shy girls fear, and a blush had taken over her face.

"My lady, I have seen you naked before. Why do you hide from me now?" he had asked in a voice that had concerned her, and, excited her. She had looked to him and the look in his eyes excited her even more. He moved the towel slightly as he took a step closer. "Come my Lady, I will dry you." His voice had continued to be soft, and exciting. She had watched him, unsure of what she should do, when she realized that she had already stood, and was walking to the waiting towel, and him.

Her smile grew as she remembered how her blush covered her entirely, and that had been all that did, as she left the water. Her surprising modesty had wanted her to cover herself with her hands, but her excitement had held her hands to her sides. She remembered looking into his eyes, and watching as they traveled her body. Her excitement had grown continually. By the time the towel touched her, her breathing was already ragged. She remembered when his hands, holding the towel, had begun to caress the lake water from her, her head had lulled back and she had begun to pant quietly. When the towel had finished its work, and had been discarded, his hands had made contact with her flesh, she had begun to tremble. When his face had again come in front of hers, she had lost what little control she had. Throwing her arms around his neck, her lips had crashed into his, and they had gone to the ground. Later, with the warmth of her passion still holding her, her head on his chest, her leg drawn up on him, and his arms around her, she had stopped caring about anything, but her love of him. Silence had closed in around them as they shared the love that they had finally accepted. She then remembered that the first surprising meeting with the Queen, had come as she had lain in Ralsanac's arms.

<hr />

"I have been wondering how long it would take you two to consummate your love," a female voice had said gently. Cartope almost laughed as she remembered how she and Ralsanac gasped, as they tried to cover their nakedness. They had looked up at a woman and a man, who stood just a short distance from them. Their meager clothing, a simple short cape, that was fastened around their necks and draped casually over their right shoulders left their upper torsos bared. The very small cloths, that were in front and back, did very little, if anything, to hide their lower body. Their gender was very obvious to the two on the ground. The woman had wore some kind of adornment on her head, and a very strange amulet around her neck. They both were very beautiful of face, and body. Cartope remembered how she could not help but feel envy of the woman.

"Who are you?' Cartope had asked, as soon as she had been able to find her voice. The woman had smiled.

"I am Queen Neponities, and this," she had said, and indicated the male with her; "is my Chosen Mate, Traredonar," she had told them, holding her gentle smile. "You are in the Central Section, the largest of three sections on our world of Neponia," she had added. As much as she had tried not to, Cartope had not been able to stop herself from glancing at the exposed, well formed males lower body. She had glanced to Ralsanac, and saw that he had a small grin as he looked over the female. She had jabbed him in the ribs, and he had looked at her in surprise. "It would be much easier to talk with you if you were standing," the Queen had told them. Ralsanac and Cartope had looked to each other. "Do not fear your nakedness. We are not ashamed, or embarrassed, of our bodies. You do not need to worry of our eyes." The Queen had said. She had held her gentle smile as she spoke. Cartope had shrugged and grinned. She had then risen, and faced the two. Ralsanac had stood as well, but Cartope had had to chuckle that he had held his hands together, low in front of him. The woman had not looked at his body, but she had looked at Cartope's. So had the man. She did chuckle as she remembered that she had blushed for the interest of both of their looks. "You are very attractive Cartope," Neponities had said softly. Cartope had looked to her.

"How did you know my name?" she had asked, with concern. The woman continued to smile.

"We have been watching, and listening, to your kind since your arrival on Neponia," she had told her, and then looked over Ralsanac. "I feel that your mating will bring a child, a male," she had added. Cartope chuckled again, that she had blushed deeper, with the thought that they had been watched. Neponities had extended her hand to Cartope. "Come, let us find a place of comfort, and talk of the future of our two peoples," she had said. Cartope had easily accepted Neponities hand, and they had walked to a shaded log. The men had followed. The two women had then begun working out an agreement for their shared living on Neponia.

It was during that conference that Cartope, and Ralsanac, had learned that Neponia was a female dominant society. The women were the only ones to possess magical talents. They were the ones who controlled everything, and although rare, they were not above sharing mates, or each other, when the mood struck them. Cartope and the women of her group, had felt right at home. Of course, a child's parental history was kept close track of.

It was also then that they had learned the name of the large canine creatures, that had preyed on them, when they had first come here. They had built their homes in the trees, to be safe from the nightly hunts of the Gorgamins, that had cost three of their numbers. They also learned of another race, called Mearlies. The Mearlies were small, just three feet tall, and they reminded Cartope strongly of Elves.

Now, many years later, after many children, most of who mated with the local peoples, Cartope and her people had adopted the clothing, and life style, of those of Neponia. Then, without warning, Cartope's relaxation was interrupted by her daughter and granddaughter. Nepopea, Cartope's only daughter, and Seastaria, her granddaughter from Nepopea and her Chosen Mate Draretonar, and at not yet two, was a powerful seer and talker, came to Cartope, and told her of a coming danger. Cartope listened to the girl, and then sent her daughter to tell Neponities of Seastaria's warning. Cartope and Neponities met hours later, and began their planning against the seen bandits invasion. Barsynia listened to their plotting. Later, she reported all she had heard, to her King, Somora.

<hr />

It was the afternoon, the day after the attack on Zentler, and Edward came from the office he had only recently inherited, heading for the conference room. The other three Keepers of Magic of Vistalin had arrived, and were now waiting for him there. They were all very concerned of this new threat to all of the domains. He entered the room, and the buzz of conversation quieted. He took his place at the head of the table, closest to the door. The history of how he came to be sitting in this place, flashed through his mind, as he settled in his chair.

His great grandmother, Marie, had been named Keeper of all Magic of Vistalin, and the title was accepted by any that took the position of Keeper of Magic, for the North West domain. He was still slightly uncomfortable being called the Keeper of all Magic of Vistalin. Especially since both Prestilon, the Keeper of Magic for the North

East Domain, and Norson, the Keeper of Magic for the South East Domain, were in fact, stronger in magic than he.

Carla, his wife, sat at the other end of the table. She now smiled softly at him. Edward could not forget that both of these chairs, had only days earlier, had been occupied by his parents. He glance to the other three Keepers, who sat on the right side of the table from him, and their wives', who sat opposite of them. His eyes quickly scanned the many attending this conference, which included Quoslon and Xanalenor, his parents. He saw that the gathered witnesses completely filled the room. All eyes, and ears, were centered on him. Edward allowed his eyes to travel from one to the next, of those who sat at the table. From a Keeper, to their wife, to the next Keeper, and wife. When he reached the eyes of his wife, he returned her smile.

"I have talked with the Overseer, as well as Semotor of Ventoria, Jarsalon of Dolaris, Croldena of Corsendora, Crendoran of Calisonnos, and Quansloe and Gordon, of the Plain and Zentler," Edward started his talk. There were nods of understanding by all at the table, and the room. "There is no doubt of these bandits existence, and, that they possess magical powers." He saw the worried looks exchanged by just about everyone in the room. "It would also seem, that they are in possession of Amplifying Stones." A murmur broke out, throughout the room. Edward held up his hand, and quiet settled. He again looked to each at the table. "Each of us have had seers, who have seen different parts of what had happened in Zentler, and we each have our opinions of what must be done about it." He held up the parchments that each of the Keepers had given him earlier. Again nods were made, but there were several eyes around the table, and room, that had taken on a very hard expressions. "Mentalon, Carla, Glornina, and many others', are searching to find anything they can find out about these assailants." Smiles joined the nods. "For now, all we can do to prepare for them, is to start to work with our defenses, especially our armies, and to teach all how to get to places of safety quickly, especially our daughters." He saw that there were several looks of unhappiness aimed at him.

"Until we know more about them, there is very little that can be done directly," Edwards voice got louder. "To rush off in all directions, because of anger, or fear, would be playing directly into these terrorists hands," he added, holding the volume to his voice. He did not look at only those at the table, but to all in the room, as he had spoke. His expression showed his controlled anger, as he too fought his own desires. Finally he saw the nods of understanding he wanted. He looked to the three Keepers at the table. "Is there anything you wish to add?" he asked them. Prestilon raised his hand.

"I agree with your idea concerning our working on defenses," Prestilon stated. "I also want to add that I think that we must also maintain a communication system with as many of the outer fringe domains, as can be done. I recommend that a panel of talkers, a few from each, of the strongest domains, be formed, and those communications be established." Edward led those at the table, and around the room, with nods of agreement.

"I agree Prestilon, good idea." Edward looked first to Carla, then to the other wives'. "I believe you ladies are more familiar with the talkers of your domains. Would you be able to arrange this panel, together?" All four women nodded to him, as they smiled knowingly to each other. Edward nodded. "Is there anything else?' he asked, as he looked to those at the table, then around the room. Paolaria stood, seemingly unaffected by the fact that she was nursing her second child when she stood. "What is it Paolaria?" Edward asked, doing his best not to look at the child she held to her chest.

"If they do indeed possess Amplifying Stones, that would mean that there has to be another source to the stones. Is there anyone, in any of the domains, who could locate that source?" she asked, and then sat, switching the baby to her other breast after sitting. Edward stared at her. Not because for a split second, her upper torso was completely bare, in a very crowded room, but because she had asked a question that no one else, including himself, seemed to have thought of. Edward turned to those at the table, and saw the same wide eyed expressions. He turned back to Paolaria.

"I don't know Paolaria, but you have just raised a very interesting thought. One I guarantee that I am going to find out about, thank you." The young woman smiled, nodded, and then went back to her baby. He looked to all at the table. "I believe we have our directions. Would the Keepers please come with me. The rest of you can start to work on what must be done." Edward stood, ending the meeting. Carla came to him and took his arm.

"I've told the ladies to begin working on their ideas for the panel. I'm coming with you," she told him, and he was smart enough not to argue.

"So am I," Quoslon said, with Xanalenor at his side. Edward nodded, as he led them all to the office. No one noticed the one who casually walked to a secluded part of the castle, smiling.

⁓⋯⊙⧫⊙⋯⁓

Namson listened to Edward's report, via the orb. He too raised his brows when Edward brought up Paolaria's question. "I never thought of that Edward," Namson said softly, as he looked to Glornina, who was sitting on the couch, and had been listening in. He saw that her eyes were wide as well. She shrugged to him and then lifted the index finger of her right hand. He could see that she was thinking. He knew that meant that she was talking with someone, about something. "We will check on that and get back to you all," he told the Keeper of all Magic of Vistalin, breaking the connection. Namson watched his wife. At first she smiled, but then frowned. She nodded and looked to Namson.

"Meritilia says, that Perolon said, that there was a special gift that only few elves had ever possessed, that allowed them to locate stones that have the proper qualities to be a magical medium. He also told her, that as there has been no great surge to find new stones, he doesn't know if any of the elves alive, now possess that skill anymore." Namson still watched her, for she was not looking at him, but inward. "He said that he would get back to me about the matter." Her voice had begun to get softer, and softer, as she spoke. Her brows knitted as she thought.

"What are you thinking so hard about?' he asked, as he came and sat down next to her, on the couch.

"Great grandpa Mike told me something, when he had shown me the Amplifying Stone, that not many realized, and I am trying to remember what it was," she screamed, quietly, fighting her own memory. He smiled and put his arm around her shoulder.

"When there is something I can't remember, I try to not think about it, and it comes to me," he told her softly. She slowly turned her head and looked at him as though he had lost his good sense. Without any warning, her eyes flew wide.

"That's it!" she cried out, turning all the way to him, grabbing his leg with both of her hands, much harder than he thought was needed.

"What?" he asked, trying not to wince too much.

"He told me the story of when his cousin Candy, used her communication crystal to find her twin brother, Willy!" she told him. It was his turn to wonder of her sanity. She shook her head, seeing the look he gave her. "He told me that by holding the communication stone in her hand, that she wore on a chain around her neck, thinking of Willy, saying his name, and the word, *Find*, the stone led her to locate Willy! He also said that he could not think of any reason that any magical stone would not work the same way, if someone was looking for a stone like it." It was Namson's turn to lift his brows.

"Do you mean that we could use the Amplifying Stone I have, to locate other Amplifying Stones?" he asked quietly. She looked back at him, and shrugged.

"You got a better idea?" she asked with a half grin. Namson looked at her and shrugged. He then spelled the Amplifying Stone that Mike had stored in the hidden vault, to him. He then called Perolon, the leader of the elfin world, using the orb, as Glornina looked the stone over.

Later that night, after the stone had been returned to the safety of the hidden vault from which it had been spelled, Glornina, unable to sleep, lay listening to her husband's gentle snoring, thinking of how to use the stone to find more, when a voice came to her mind. It had been a very long time since she had heard the voice, and there was a tremor of concern that passed through her.

⋙•━☆✦☆❖✦☆•⋘

"Hello Mistress of The Realm. I call you now, for it is time that we meet, face to face," Cartope told her. "I ask that just you and I meet at this time, for the domain I now reside in, is led by a peoples that are female dominate, and I'm not sure how the Overseer would affect our hostesses." Glornina thought rapidly. Cartope had lived up to her oath of never bothering the Realm, or any of the domains. Glornina felt that there was a sincerity to her voice, that caused Glornina to trust her words.

"When, and where?" she asked calmly.

"Tomorrow, I will bring you to us. Just let me know when you are free of others," Cartope said. "Do not fear. I swear that you can freely return to the Realm, at any time you want, but I ask that you hear us out first."

"I will let you know when I am free Cartope," Glornina said, and broke the connection. She turned her head, and looked to her husband's profile. She wondered what he would say about what she was about to do. She didn't like the answer.

Gordon was very happy that his house had been spared the torches of the bandits. He was also glad that they could use the house to shelter as many of the citizens of Zentler as they had, but he was not real happy about the loss of privacy. He held Xanaporia, her back to him, as they lay on the mattress on the floor. His bed, which he missed dearly, and was only a few feet from him, was now occupied by two elderly couples who couldn't get down to, or up from the floor, easily. He knew that the entire house was filled with people. Every square inch of floor space. Every couch, large chair, or anything else that could hold a sleeping body, was filled. His only comfort was knowing that every house, building, or shed, that had not been burned, was packed as completely as this one.

His mind went back over the plans that had been made that day, at the meeting that all of the town had attended. A salvage crew had been formed. They were assigned to try and save any boards that could be used, or anything else of value that could be found. A planning crew, the ones to design common buildings for eating, sleeping, or whatever, as well as the managing of the many volunteers for the different work crews, had been formed. The farmers, from all of the surrounding farms, had begun to bring food, milk, and anything else they thought could fill a need. Thankfully, that including blankets, clothes, and the other things, that for all of lives of the peoples of Zentler, had been taken for granted, but now were very crucial. Considering that only one day had passed since the attack, Gordon was pleased with their efforts.

"We must sleep, my love," Xanaporia whispered, informing him that she knew he did not sleep. He smiled, and squeezed her just slightly.

"I'm trying my love, I'm trying," he whispered back. She snuggled even tighter to him.

"I am proud of the way you have led the people," she told him, and went to sleep, leaving him with a smile of pride, and a blush of modesty. He soon found that sleep could come to him, and he let it.

───── ⋙⋆⋆⋆⋙⋆⋆⋆⋙ ─────

Semotor, great grandson of Roulitor and Pielsakor, and now the General of the Armies of Ventoria, looked to those gathered at the table, and around the large meeting room of the General of the Armies palace. His eyes settled on Calsorack, the young Governor of Bendine Island.

"What does Bendine plan?" he asked simply. Semirack's grandson returned his look, and smiled, with only one side of his mouth.

"There are many who think, that as with Castope, we go after them," he said quietly. The General of the Armies, maintaining his eye contact, nodded.

"And your thoughts?" he asked, his voice calm. Calsorack held his half grin, and shrugged, slightly, with only his right shoulder.

"We know not where to go. I think that we should learn more first, then make our choices," Calsorack stated, his voice as calm as Semotor's. Semotor nodded.

"These are my thoughts as well. I have been talking with the Overseer, the Keepers of Vistalin, Jarsolan, Crendora, and Croldena, and they all agree." There were nods from all, but a few who still wore angry looks. "All domains prepare their armies, and there is a communications network being put into operation, that we will be joining. For now, that is all that can be done until the base these bandits use, has been found." Semotor watched all those present, and saw that some were very prepared to speak their opinions of what must be done. "There is no reason to go chasing ghosts!" he told them all, his voice gaining volume. "It would spread our forces far too thin, and gain virtually nothing!" His voice had taken on a commanding tone with the volume, as his eyes slowly swept the room. The dissenters did not challenge that tone, or his glare. With a final nod of his head, Semotor rose, ending the meeting. He watched as the rest in the room, followed his lead, and rose from their chairs. They left for their respective duties, each small group in their own discussions. When all had left, his wife Tererence came to him, placing her hand on his arm.

"I am afraid of some of them," she told him, referring to certain members of the council who had just left. He smiled, and pulled her into his arms.

"Do not worry my love," he told her gently. "I know who to watch, and they will follow my lead, simply because there are too many others' that will make them." She sighed. He pulled his head back, and looked to her questioning.

"Both Borserence and Drurence are pregnant, again," she told him speaking of their daughter, and daughter-in-law, and then chuckled. He grinned.

"Haven't they figured out what causes that yet?" he asked her. They both laughed as they left the meeting room, their arms around each other's waist. Neither saw Barsantorack watching them from a nearby alcove, nor the evil little grin that came to his very fat face. They also missed the Bendine sneaking off to another part of the General of the Armies palace.

Pinsikar raced from Telposar's door. The human scared him more than he wanted to admit. He wanted to check on a few things at his office, which was simply a small room, built on the side of his hovel, which was a distance from the castle. As he neared his hovel, he saw that Pestikar, one of the spies who worked for him, and one of the largest, at over five foot tall, waited outside of the office for him. Pestikar was watching Daridar, Pinsikar's second oldest daughter, as she worked in the small garden behind the hovel "If you want her, make your bid," Pinsikar said as he opened the door.

"You don't pay enough for me to bid on any female," Pestikar stated as he followed Pinsikar into the office.

"To bad," Pinsikar said. "What have you learned?" Pestikar laughed a high pitched Dwarf laugh.

"You were right. Porkligor and Rentaring plot something," Pestikar said. Pinsikar looked at him, and his eyes flared angrily.

"What?" Pinsikar roared at him. "What do they plot?" Pestikar glared back at him.

"I only heard few real words, but I did hear Brandaro's name, and they were sneering when they said it." Pinsikar scowled at him.

"That is all?" he asked, and Pestikar glared back at him.

"They sat in that damned corner booth. It was hard to get near them without being seen," he told his boss, and there was anger in his whining voice. "And I bid these for Daridar," he added, holding out his hand with some jewels in it, as well as some pieces of gold. Pinsikar looked at what Pestikar held, and wondered where he had gotten that much.

"Add your next month's wages, and I accept," Pinsikar said. Pestikar glared harder. He looked out the window at Daridar, and then back to Pinsikar.

"Done," he said, and put the things he had been holding, on the desk. Pinsikar nodded and went to the door that led into the hovel, and opened it.

"Dormadar, gather Daridar's things together. Pestikar has just bid her!" He shut the door before he heard all of her whiny answer. Through the window, he saw Daridar look up, for she had heard his call to her mother. When she turned, and started for the back door of the hovel, carrying what she had already picked, Pinsikar saw the grin the girl tried to hide. Pinsikar gathered the valuables from the desk, and then looked to Pestikar. "Find out what the two plot," he ordered, and waved him from his office. Pestikar nodded as he went out the door. He turned towards the front door of the hovel. Pinsikar heard the sounds as Pestikar took possession of Daridar. Pinsikar was relieved that he would no longer have to feed her, but he would miss that girl. She was the only one of his four daughters that had ever shown any indication of pleasure, when he used her.

CHAPTER TWO

Glornina appeared, and four things immediately stood out to her. The first being the striking beauty of the small pasture area she had appeared in. The second was that the woman before her was virtually naked. The third was that the man who stood beside her, wore no more than she did, and the fourth, and most surprising thing, was that they both wore Amplifying Stones around their necks.

"Mistress of the Realm, I am Cartope," the woman said simply. Glornina did her best to ignore the fact that the short cape over her shoulder, and the very small piece of cloth worn over her pelvic area, did absolutely nothing to hide her body. She didn't even try to look at the man, for his meager coverings did even less to hide his anatomy.

"My name is Glornina," she replied, keeping her eyes on the woman's. Cartope nodded and smiled softly.

"I am happy to finally meet you," Cartope said. "Come, let's sit in the shade, and talk. The Queen should be here shortly." Cartope pointed to three chairs that had been placed in the shade of a very large tree. "This is my

Chosen Mate Ralsanac," she said, and indicated the man beside her. Glornina looked to his eyes and nodded. "If it would make you more comfortable," Cartope said as she led them to the chairs. "We could spell clothes to ourselves, or, you could remove yours." There was a hint in the tone of Cartope's voice that Glornina did not like.

"I'm fine, thank you," Glornina said as she sat down. "Now, what did you want to talk about?' she asked, noticing that Ralsanac did not sit, but stood to the side, near Cartope. Cartope smiled slightly.

"I had hoped to have the Queen here when we talked," she said. As if cued, a tall, lovely, and shapely woman, and a well muscled man, walked up, wearing the same style of clothing. Glornina immediately saw that the woman was the only one of the two wearing an Amplifying Stone. Adding to Glornina's discomfort was the fact that the man's very limited clothing, who accompanied the Queen, didn't cover as much of him as the first ones. Nudity was not new to her, considering the imps, the occasional meeting of people in and out of the bathing rooms, and the swimming at that lake west of Realm City, where everybody went naked, but this was a different situation, and she was glad that she had come alone. She was quite sure that Namson would be eyeing the two very attractive women, with more than a casual look.

"I am here Cartope," the woman said, and Cartope stood. Glornina followed her lead. The woman looked Glornina up and down quickly, and smiled gently. "You must be the Mistress of the Realm," she said softly. Glornina nodded. "I am Neponities, Queen of the Central Section of Neponia," she said almost casually. "It would seem that we have a common enemy, and Cartope thought that it would be to our advantage to have your kind help us in combating it," the Queen said with that same gentle smile, and her eyes again traveled Glornina. Glornina glanced at Cartope, and then back to the Queen.

"I am not sure what you mean by that, but I am here to listen," she said as calmly as she could, for she saw that both men were giving her form a critical eyeing. Apparently the Queen saw the same thing, and that it was making Glornina uncomfortable.

"Traredonar, Ralsanac, why don't you both bring us something cool to drink, and remember your manners when you return," she told them, with a commanding tone in her voice. Both men bowed slightly, and walked off. "Please, let us sit," Neponities suggested, her voice back to the gentleness of before. The three women sat in the chairs, and Cartope started the conversation.

The reason I have asked you here, is that my granddaughter, Seastaria, who is a very powerful seer, came to me and told me that assailants would come to this section of Neponia, and they would kill, rape, and steal. They would capture many to sell as slaves on their home world," Cartope said, keeping her voice a steady tone. Glornina blinked several times before she could think of the proper words to reply. Cartope didn't give her the chance. "She also told me that a village, near the domain called the Plain, had just recently been attacked." Glornina could only nod. "I know that the Plain is a very dear part of the Realms coalition, so I thought if the Realm were to help us, we could repel these monsters, and, possibly rid all of their horror." Glornina stared at her for a moment, and then looked to the Queen. Cartope drew her attention back. "Queen Neponities, perhaps if you were to tell her what you have told me, she could better understand ours, and their, needs," Cartope said. Glornina again looked to the tall Queen, who sat, her back board straight, in her chair. The gentle, but somehow disturbing smile, had not left the Queens lips.

"Many years ago, when I was still but a very young girl, barely able to walk, bandits attacked the Northern Section." Neponities started her telling. "They were led by a huge man. It is said that he had a lad with him who was also quite large. They were ruthless, and killed many of that section. Men and women were captured and taken, as well as many other men killed, and women raped, and tortured. They also took a large chest of our power stones." The Queen touched the amulet around her neck. "It was about fifteen years later that a second, smaller band, tried to attack this section, but my mother had learned from the first attack, and easily defeated them. In the few survivors, there were some of the bandits slaves. Among them, we found a woman from our Northern Section, all but dead from the abuse she had received in those fifteen years. The stories she told of the abuses received by the women, and the horrible work, being forced to breed with other females, and beatings the men had been subject to, told us all of a horrible peoples from many different places, who made up this bandits home world." Here the Queen hesitated. Her emotions of what she remembered showing clearly in her eyes. Glornina waited for her to continue, thinking of the fate of the poor girls taken from Zentler. "The poor woman had only lived a little longer than a week before she died. We learned from her telling, and we believe that those coming, are from that same world." Neponities looked intently onto Glornina's eyes.

"Do you have more of those stones?" Glornina asked, pointing to the amulet the Queen wore. The Queen nodded, after a glance to Cartope. Glornina was not sure of what she was to do now. "We call those stones Amplifying Stones, for they multiply the powers of the wearer. It was thought that there were no more than the one my husband, the Overseer of the Realm, possessed, and the few that we were able to make into collars for those who fought the evils of the Dark Magic." Cartope nodded with a half grin.

"So, that is how you were so easily able to defeat Castope, and the Dark City," she said softly, looking at Glornina. The Mistress of the Realm looked to her with no happiness in her eyes.

"Very little of the success of that attack was caused by the Amplifying stones, but they were a large part of the defeat of Palakrine," she told Cartope. Cartope stared at her for a moment, losing her grin.

"Cartope had told me of these events," Neponities said. "I had doubted her somewhat, concerning the power of which she spoke, but I see now that her words were true." The Queen turned her eyes to Cartope. "Please forgive me my doubts," she asked of Cartope, and Cartope smiled her forgiveness. She turned her eyes back to Glornina. "What level of power is possessed in this Realm of yours?" she asked, and Glornina heard a tone of worry in her voice. Glornina did not smile as she returned the Queens look.

"There are a large number who do not need the Amplifying Stones, especially my husband, the Overseer of the Realm," she told the Queen. Neponities eyes opened wider as the two men returned, with three tall mugs on trays. After they had handed the women the mugs, and had stepped back, Neponities, who Glornina had seen quickly recover from Glornina's announcement, was thinking. The Queen took a sip from the mug and then looked to Glornina.

"As Mistress of the Realm, are you one of those who do not need the stones?" she asked carefully. Cartope was also staring at Glornina. Glornina took the mug from her lips after her sip, surprised at the wonderful taste, and the realization that there was some sort of liquor in the drink. She returned the Queens look, and nodded once. The Queens eyes never left hers. "Could you perhaps give me a demonstration of this power you claim?" she asked Glornina calmly.

"What would you need?" Glornina asked her. The Queen looked around.

"That tree, the one that stands out from the rest." Glornina looked to the tall tree the Queen pointed to, and saw that it was an easy three hundred feet away. "Could you cause it to fall from where you are?" Glornina returned her eyes to the Queens.

"I see no reason to destroy a tree, but yes," she told her. The Queen smiled, and Glornina easily saw that the Queen was thinking that a blast spell would be too far spread to accomplish the results she asked for. The tree was much too thick.

"Neponia is mostly covered in woods, besides, we can always find a use for the wood," she told Glornina quietly. The Mistress of the Realm glanced at Cartope, and saw her eyes narrowed slightly, and questioning. She looked back to the Queen, and shrugged as she nodded.

"Very well," she said and only lifted her right hand, extending only her index finger. The Queens right brow lifted as she saw her simple maneuvers. Glornina whispered, and gave a quick twitch with her finger, downward, and to the right. The Queen jerked her eyes to the tree. For just a moment it stood as before, and then, the trunk slid from the stump, cut at a downward angle, hitting the ground, which caused the tree to fall with a very loud crash. Traredonar ran for the tree. He stopped next to it, stared at it for a moment, and then turned and ran back. Glornina tried to ignore the fact that as Traredonar ran, the front flap he wore, which hadn't cover him very well to start with, now flapped up with the efforts of his running. She didn't want to admit that the sight was pleasant to watch. Traredonar stopped next to the Queen, not even breathing hard from his efforts.

"My Lady, not even a saw, in the hands of our best woodsmen, could have cut as smoothly, or as evenly," he stated, and he looked to Glornina, and there was definite concern in his eyes. The Queen looked at him for a moment, and then turned to Glornina. Her eyes were wider than before. Glornina quickly glanced to Cartope, and saw that she still looked to the fallen tree, and her eyes were also wide, as she returned her look to Glornina. There was a moment or two of silence before the Queen spoke again.

"You say there are many that have this kind of power?" she asked Glornina quietly. Glornina slowly nodded several times, never taking her eyes from the Queens. Neponities and Cartope shared astonished looks. It was then that Nepopea and Seastaria came running to them.

"Grandma," Seastaria called as she neared. "There is another domain that faces danger! The Plain!" she finished as the two came to a stop near Cartope. Both Neponities and Cartope, looked to Glornina, as she called to her husband. Fifty feet away, Barsynia reported to her King that the Realm would now be aiding Neponia.

⸻

Prelilian, the wife of Tarson, General of the Realm Armies, stood on the rear terrace of the palace. She knew that Glornina had assigned her this duty, because Prelilian actually knew the talkers of the Realm better than Glornina did, and she had told Prelilian that she had something else of importance she had to do that morning. The wives' of the Keepers of Magic of Vistalin, Carla, the North West, Pentilian, the South West, Jarsillia, the North East, and Aliena, the South

East, appeared first. They were quickly followed by Tererence of Ventoria, Quentoria of Dolaris, Meladiana of Corsendora, and Michele of Calisonnos. For several minutes there was the welcoming of meeting friends. It was Carla that brought them all back to the responsibilities they had gathered for.

"Ladies," there were several short chuckles from the others, for they were all still quite young. Carla smiled as well, as she continued. "We had better get this panel of talkers working. All of the domains are depending on us." Her words were quiet, but they all knew the importance of them.

"I recommend at least three talkers from each domain," Aliena said, and several others nodded.

"What about a domain that does not have a talker?" Pentilian asked quietly, and then looked to each of the other women. "How are we to warn them, or help them?" They all looked to her, and then to each other.

"I don't want to sound hard hearted, but until that domain, or domains, are found, there really is nothing we can do for them," Prelilian said softly. They looked to each other, and knew the truth of her words. "Now let's start with the idea of three from each domain and see what we can come up with." There were nods by all, and the ladies sat at the large table that had been placed there for them, and began to prepare the workings of the panel. It was finally decided that Carla would be the leader of the panel, as she was actually the strongest talker, and in magical talent, of those present. There would be four talkers from each Domain. One of the four would be a more powerful talker, and that those would take turns to act as a central controller for the panel. The other three would take their turns, covering a full day and night with the talkers of the panel. One of the duties for all of the panel, would be searching for yet unknown domains, hoping that one would tell them of these bandits home.

<hr>

Namson listened to his wife's telling with patience, and anger.

Daridar listened to the voices she had suddenly started hearing, as she basked the warmth of the pleasure Pestikar had given her.

Isabella turned from the groping of the three laughing bandits, without a sound. She forced herself into a corner of the cage they were locked into, where, with all the other girls, it was not worth their effort to try and touch her body. She had already tried to spell her and the girls back to Zentler, but the bandits must have placed a shield around them, for she couldn't. She had tried to unbind them, and open the cage to free them, but for some reason she didn't understand, she couldn't. She listened to the cries and whimpering of the other girls that were being held with her, bound as she was, unable to stop the gropings. The occasional sound of tearing cloth was heard as the men tried to get to their flesh. Tears of rage came to her eyes. She felt that the men knew they could not rape these girls for that would lessen their value when they would be brought to the slave sales, but they were intent on having as much fun with them as they could. She began her simple spell, silently. Even with her hands bound behind her, she made each of the men feel the pain that stopped their assaults. As they were not the smartest of individuals, they had no idea what had caused their pains. She thought of Melsikan. That gentle, shy boy, who had awoken her heart, and desires. She thought of the sunny afternoon, in the small glen in the woods, where they had shared those pleasures. Would he ever accept her again, after what she knew these beasts planned? Her tears of anger were now joined with tears of heartache.

Daridar now decided to answer the calling voices.

Namson began to realize the danger in Glornina's words, and the value of the finding of the second source of Amplifying Stones.

<hr />

Penny came out the back door of the house, on the ranch that was still called the Zentler Ranch, but was now owned by Paul, the youngest son of Jenny and Davian, and the father of her husband, Morsley. She carried the large capped, container of lemonade to the buggy that waited by the porch She was bringing this for her husband, and the five men who worked with him. She was proud that Morsley and his father, were trying to do all they could for the victims of Zentler. As she drove the buggy near, she could hear the sounds of the lumber mill where Morsley and the others, worked to get as many boards as they could from the trees they had fell that morning. As she stopped the buggy, and then climbed down, she heard Morsley call to another man named Randy.

"Get some water in the reservoir before that blade snaps!" Morsley called, and Randy said he was on it. Almost instantly after Randy's reply, there came a loud twang, followed by a scream of someone in the mill. This was followed by everybody yelling orders. She could easily hear their panic in their yelling. She forgot what she had brought, and ran into the building. She looked around as she entered, and saw Morsley disappear below the conveyer, that carried the cut boards. She actually dived over the conveyer, and landed next to her husband. Morsley was trying to stop the thrashings of Randy, a big man that with too much drink would turn to the mean side, but without drink, was one of the kindest men in Zentler. She scrambled, and pinned the leg that sprayed blood from the severing below the knee. She managed to stop the pumping blood from the leg, and put a calming spell on Randy. Morsley looked around quickly, to see if any had seen his wife perform her magical remedies, and was happy to see that none had, for they all worked at stopping the blade that was still being pulled by the drive wheel. Some yelling at the searing heat that had caused the blade to snap. Morsley looked to Penny, and spelled the blood of Randy from her, and around them. "The heat of the blade cauterized the leg as it cut through," he told her in a hoarse whisper. She nodded, and finished sealing the severed leg. The problem they had was, when they looked at Randy, he stared back at them, and his eyes told them that he had seen what they had done.

"We will explain later," Penny told him as she tried to wrap the severed leg. She looked to his widened eyes. "Please, do not speak of what has been done, please," she begged of him, and he looked to Morsley.

"This is going to be one hell of a explanation," he whispered, and then looked to his leg. "Oh god damn!" he roared, and grabbed at his shortened leg, as he fainted.

"She is a strong magical power my husband, and she will survive this terror that has taken her," Xanaporia whispered as she came to Gordon. He was looking at the destroyed house of Isabella, and her mother Ava, who had been killed during the bandits raid. He didn't look at her as his heart raced.

"You knew?" he asked simply. She put her arm through his, with a small sigh.

"Yes, I knew," she told him. "Ava was a very pretty young woman, and you were drinking quite heavily then. It did not take much to realize that you had taken her to the Valley, and hid her until Isabella's birth. I found out that your many visits to the Valley were not all social, especially when no one there had known you had visited." He turned to look at her, and she smiled softly. "You have always shown your love for me and the children, and you stopped your association with Ava, and stopped your drinking, so I did not say anything. You made a mistake, and you made the efforts to correct what you could, and, I know you have not strayed since." She looked into his eyes. "I know you love me, and I know you regret your moment of weakness," she told him. Tears came to his eyes as he took her into his arms. "I also know that you have love for the girl, as your child."

"I am so sorry my love. So very sorry," he whispered. She nodded against his cheek, fighting her own tears.

———

Porkligor was grumbling complaints as Telposar led him into the presence of Brandaro. His eyes, at least the one that was not swelled shut, immediately went to the bodies of the two women that were seated with his leader. Brandaro chuckled at the stupid actions of the obese pirate. "Lord Brandaro, why ya has me treat dis way?" Porkligor asked in a semi quiet voice. "I haf dos as ya's asked, and I los money dosing it." Telposar bent the fat man, pushing him to one knee.

"Show proper respect to your Ruler, Porkligor!" he commanded. Porkligor cried out with the pain of his knee hitting the floor. Brando didn't care as his eyes went to the females who were led into the room, their hands bound behind them, and their necks chained together. He rose from his throne, and advanced on them. Most of the girls gasped at his size, and began to cry again. All but one, and Brandaro went straight to her. Isabella's eyes never left his as she stared angrily up at him. A small grin came to his lips as he stopped in front of the defiant one, that barely came to the height of his chest. He reached out and grabbed her hair, pulling her up to her tip toes, but she did not cry out for the pain. She kept her concentration on the spell she was preparing, and her plans including taking the equipment from him, that caused his obvious desire. His smile grew as he looked into her eyes. His eyes traveled her body, seeing that very little was still covered by the tattered clothes she wore. He reached out with his other hand, and tore the remaining clothes from her, and she faced him completely naked. There was some deep growls by the many men, and the one dwarf, in the room, and he could see that she knew their thoughts. He laughed at her.

"You have power little one. That could be of use to me," he told her in his deep, and playful voice. "You plot to take from me my manhood." He bent slightly, and looked deeply onto her eyes. "Go ahead and try," he said, and spun her so her hands were to him. The other men, and dwarf, made threatening laughs as they enjoyed the front view of her body, and she cast her spell. Brandaro laughed again, and spun her back to face him. She felt real fear when she saw that her spell had had no affect on him at all. "Besaline!" Brandaro called to his female slave master.

A large woman, wearing a red band around her neck, that held a small, varying colored stone in it, stepped forward. Brandaro looked to the guards and they quickly unlocked the neck bracket, freeing Isabella from the chain. "Take this one, and prepare her as my private slave," he ordered, pulling Isabella towards the woman, by the hair. Morselia and Caratelia exchanged looks at Brandaro's command. Besaline took Isabella's hair in her large hands, and pulled the naked Isabella out of the room. Porkligor groaned loudly as he watched the girl being pulled from the room. Brandaro chuckled as he turned back to the still kneeling

Porkligor. "Do not fear Porkligor, I will pay you for her," he told the fat man as he retook his seat. He indicated that Telposar should stand the fat one. Porkligor had to put most of his weight on his other leg when the huge man pulled him up, for his aching knee wouldn't support him completely.

"Lord Brandaro," Porkligor whined. "I's los money on dis raid, dat I's mind ya's, ya's sen me on, and ya's now take da one female I mih get som of das los back." Brandaro glared at him.

"I told you I would pay you for her, and, if you tell me what I want to know, and if it is the right information, I will give a bonus that will recoup your losses, but that will include the purchase of the others' as well," Brandaro told him in a growl. Porkligor's greedy eye opened as far as it would go, and he actually smiled, as he nodded his acceptance of the deal. The other eight wide eyed girls, still hooked to the chain, gasped, and again began to whimper as they were led from the room, in the same direction Isabella had been taken.

"Ya Lord Brandaro. Wha das you wans to know?" he asked as smoothly as his voice would allow. Brandaro sat forward slightly, staring into Porkligor's eye fiercely.

"Tell me of your raid. Even if it seems unimportant, tell me everything." The fat pirate nodded rapidly, and began his telling, including the times that his bandits had been forced to repel magical spells. Porkligor received his bonus, but it was not as much as he had hoped for. This added to his resentment for Brandaro. After Brandaro had dismissed him, he went looking for Rentaring, limping with his damaged knee, and his anger built with each flash of pain from it.

Melsikan, in his usual way, worked in silence, as he carried salvaged boards from partially burned buildings being torn down. The other workers would occasionally talk to him, and he would nod, or if pushed, answered with the least number of words as possible. All that knew him, knew of his love affair with the girl Isabella. They knew that she had been taken by the bandits, and they gave their understanding to the quiet young man. He tried not to think of her, but that was an impossibility. His anger came as he thought of how he had been surprised from behind, and beaten badly, for trying to stop the taking of her. With each twinge of pain he felt, his heart, and mind, screamed at the last he saw of her. He had been forced to see her being dragged off by that mongrel of a human, who groped her as he did it. Just before he had lost consciousness, he had seen that she did not scream, but fought with determination that required a second of the bastards, to help the first.

Melsikan's thoughts shifted to when he had first come to Zentler, just over three years earlier. He had walked into town, near the coming of evening, a large pack on his back, and stopped to look around. He had seen the help wanted sign in the window of the store, and Isabella, just leaving the store with her mother, at the same time. He had been only fourteen then, though quite large for his age. He knew he wanted the job, and the girl, and he was pretty sure he could get by without the job. He had entered the store, and pulled the sign from the window. He took it to the woman behind the counter, and held it out, without a sound. She had looked to his eyes, the sign, and then his young form. He had not flinched with her examination.

"Can you read and do numbers?" the heavy woman had asked. He had seen that woman could have almost been pretty, if she had been about a hundred pounds lighter. He had nodded, and she stared at him. "Can you talk?" she had asked with a small amount of ridicule in her voice.

"Yes, I can," he had told her simply. She again looked him over, and then picked up the newspaper that lay on the counter, and held it out to him.

"Prove it," she told him. He looked to the paper, and then to her, and chuckled as he put down the sign, and took the paper.

"The city council approves Mayor Gordon's plans to develop the far south western end of the city, for housing," he started, as the woman began to scribble on something.

"Alright," the woman had said, and held out the smaller piece of paper; "add these," she told him. He set down the newspaper, and took the smaller paper, and looked at it.

"One hundred, twenty three," he had told her, as he returned his eyes to hers. Her eyes opened wider, and she snatched the paper from him. She placed it on the counter, and taking up her pencil, began to add the figures she had written down. It took a few minutes, and then she looked at him again, from head to toe, and back.

"That's right," she said softly. "How could you do that without a pencil?" she asked. He smiled.

"The same way you did," he told her simply. "Just in my head," he added. She stared at him for some time.

"Can you write?" she asked, her voice becoming quite gentle, as a smile came to her lips.

"Yes," he told her, and she nodded.

"Wage, board and a meal a day at Menirva's. My sister runs it, but only if it ain't too pricey," she told him with warning to her voice. Melsikan fought his smile successfully, and nodded. "You got any clothes that don't carry the smell of the road, and your sweat?" she asked as she sniffed at him.

"Yes, I stopped at the last river and washed some," he told her, controlling his anger at her insinuation. She nodded as she looked to the watch strung on the chain around her neck.

"Near to closing," she said, as she scribbled something on another paper. "Down the street," she said, and pointed. He looked that direction. "There's McFurgal Boarding House. Give this to Hensen, the manager, first door to the right. He'll show you to your room. Ain't much, but there's a tub up there, and you'll have to carry the water up, but be clean when you get here at seven tomorrow morning, and don't be late," she told him, handing the piece of paper to him. He took the paper nodding. He picked up the sign and handed it to her with a smile, and left the store.

When he had arrived at the boarding house, he knocked on Hensen's door, and the crabby old man read the note he handed him. Hensen was mad that he had to walk the boy up two flights of stairs, but knew what would be if he didn't show the boy everything.

"Change of sheets every Monday," Hensen had told him, as he handed the key to Melsikan. "Don't turn in your sheets and pillow case, in the bin near my door in the morning, and there won't be none clean when you get home that night, got it," the old man told him from his place in the doorway. Melsikan had nodded, and came closer. "Hot water, first floor in back. You gotta tote it up here yourself." Melsikan nodded again. "No water pressure this floor, you gotta get your water from the second floor, near the back." Hensen sneered at him.

"I got the idea Hensen," Melsikan had said, and shoved the door closed, pushing the old man out into the hall. He listened to the man's grumblings about the young not respecting the older folks, until the stairs finally cut them off. He dropped his pack, and took the large pitcher from the bowl on the stand near the door, and went and filled it, from the second floor faucet. When he returned to the room, he put his clothes away in the worn out dresser, and then went to the window that looked out over the houses that made up the north west end of town. He was very surprised to see the girl in a back yard, not three houses from the boarding house. She was taking clothes from the drying line. He watched her until she carried the basket back into the house. He knew he was hooked from that moment on. It had taken him almost two full years to talk to her when not in the store. It had not taken long after that, and they became to talk of the town with their love. Just a month ago, they had shared the culmination of their love, in a small glen in the woods. Before they had returned to town, he had asked her to marry him, and she had said yes about three hundred times in a row. He had ordered a ring as soon as he returned to the store. It had arrived, and Melsikan planned his presentation. The night of the raid, he was on his way to Isabella's house, for that presentation, when the bandits attacked. He had tried to protect her, and lost not only her, but the ring was taken from him as well. His anger boiled in him as he plotted to find her, and the ring, for he knew that no one in town knew of his history, or, his power!

Barsantorack left the meeting hall, joining the returning group of Bendine that had attended the meeting. He listened to the many conversations around him, and he thought, as the ship took them back to the island of Bendine. When they had arrived, he went straight to his home. A germ of an idea was trying to grow in his twisted, greedy, mind, and he wanted to nurse it into a real thought. Simerence, his wife, was surprised when he walked into the kitchen at that early hour. He completely ignored her, and his daughter Vestirence, as they worked on the pies that he did not know she was selling, for her own savings. She was not surprised to see him reach into the pantry for a jug of brew.

"Starting early are we?" she asked in a condemning tone.

"Quiet wife," he growled, as he took a jug from the cabinet, a mug from another cabinet, and went to his office.

"What's with him?" Vestirence whispered, knowing better than to let him hear her. Her mother snorted, and went back to kneading dough.

"You know your father," she answered as her irritation began to show, as she worked the dough. "I'm sure he has come up with another idea on how to cheat someone else out of their earnings, instead of working for them himself," she hissed the last few words. Vestirence withdrew slightly, not wanting to be part of her mother's constant harping about her father.

Barsantorack lowered his bulk into his chair behind his desk, and then poured the mug full of brew. He drank the first half of it, and sat back to let the germ grow. He liked the Bendine version of the ogres brew that had been brought to Ventoria. It was sweeter, and he did like his sweets. He simply ignored the other males who tried to laugh at him for drinking what they called a females drink. They preferred the original, more bitter, but not stronger, brew.

He thought about what had been said during the meeting, and what Semotor had said later, about knowing his enemies. He thought about the words of Calsorack, and his anger came out. "Always playing up to Semotor aren't you," he growled to the air. "Well you shouldn't even be the Governor of Bendine," he stated loudly. "Tremarack is the pure blood descendant of Borack, he should be Ruler!" Barsantorack eyes began to open wider, as the germ had begun to grow at an alarming rate. "Yes," he said louder yet, sitting forward in his chair. "Tremarack should be Ruler, not the grandson of that half blood Semirack." He downed the rest of what was in the mug, and poured it full again. He replaced the cork in the jug, and again drank half of what was in the mug. His head beginning to nod as the germ grew to full malignity. "Tremarack is the direct blood line descendant of Borack," he restated, and a grin grew with his words. He finished his drink, and stood, heading for the door. "We will see who refuses me the position I deserve, Calsorack," he stated as he left his home, for the home of Tremarack.

Penelopy and her mother, Sophia, walked from the grave of her mother's cousin, Ava. Penelopy supported her mother's arm as they walked. Sophia wept, and moaned, and not quietly. The girl tried not to let her irritations show, for her mother had, on more than one occasion, condemned and ridiculed Ava's whorish ways, and the shame that Isabella must now bear for those ways. To say nothing of the girl following in her mother's footsteps with that common storekeeper, who was an outsider! She knew her mother's behavior was now quite beyond simple hypocrisy, to say the least. Her thoughts, and worries, were with her cousin, Isabella, whom she had become very close, without her mother's knowing of course. Isabella had told her of her abilities in magic, her love for Melsikan, and the pleasures they had shared in the glen. Penelopy had listened to her words with an envy that surprised her, and yet, did not. She hoped that Marcus would someday show his love for her, and though she would not admit it to even Isabella, hoped that she too could visit that glen, with him. She smiled as she thought of him, hiding the smile from her mother, for her mother did not approve of Marcus either. They had been forced to meet secretly, whenever they could meet. Suddenly, her mother stopped, and stiffened, causing Penelopy to look up, right into the eyes of the one in her thoughts, Marcus.

"What are you doing here?" Sophia asked in a tone that left no doubt of her contempt for the lad. His face clouded with anger.

"Mother!" Penelopy screamed. "He lost both his parents from the attack! How could you dare to ask that of him?"

"Don't you think you can talk to me like that!" Sophia ordered her harshly, and turned back to Marcus. "Why were your people buried with the rightful citizens of Zentler?" she screamed at him, and he advanced. The flowers he carried now hung from his hand, barely.

"You may think you're something quite special Mrs. Barnes, but I guarantee you that you're nothing but a loud mouthed bitch, with nothing to offer, but your contempt of all the decent people of this town!" he roared at her. Sophia screeched and shook her fist at him.

"I'm going to talk to the Sheriff, and have you arrested for talking to me like that," she screamed at him, and stormed off. Penelopy let go of her arm so as not to be dragged with her. She watched her mother walk off, and then looked to Marcus.

"I'm sorry," he told her as he came closer; "but she had no right to say that to me." She nodded, as tears came to her eyes. She closed the distance to him, and he took her into his arms. For several seconds, nothing was said between them. "Penelopy," he said into her ear, his voice very gentle; "you do know that I love you, don't you?" She jerked her head from his chest, and looked into his eyes. Her heart beat as though to jump from her chest.

"Do you, really?" she asked in a whisper. His eyes smiled with his lips, as he nodded.

"More than breath itself," he told her, and her tears of happiness flowed. She went back into his arms.

"And I love you Marcus, more than breath itself," she told him, and his arms tightened around her. They stood there, holding each other, oblivious of the people who passed them, bringing flowers, and tears to those they had lost as well. The passing people smiled at them, for many knew of their secret love, and knew of Sophia's tendencies to think herself, and thusly, her daughter, much better than most.

"Despite your mother, will you marry me Penelopy?" Marcus asked her ear softly. She again jerked her head from his chest, and nodded.

"Oh yes, yes, yes!" she declared, and went back into his arms. After a few moments, he gently pushed her from him, and went down to one knee. He pulled a small box from his vest pocket, and opened it to her. The people, who had come to visit their lost ones, now formed a circle around the two. There were smiles, and tears, looking at the young lovers. Marcus lifted the ring from the box, and took Penelope's left hand. She was trembling so much, he had difficulty getting the ring on her finger. He stood, and kissed her, just as Sophia's screech penetrated the congratulations that the people had begun to shout. They all turned to look at the approaching Sophia, who had the unwilling Sheriff in tow. They all could also see the mayor and his wife in close pursuit.

"Sheriff!" Sophia screamed at the top of her lungs. "You will arrest that hooligan for his disrespect of honest citizens, and for the obvious attempt to rape my daughter!" The was a collective gasp by all those gathered. "Penelopy, get away from that riffraff this instant," Sophia ordered as she stopped, much to the relief of the Sheriff, who had been doing everything he could to keep from being pulled off his feet. Sophia pointed at Marcus. "Get your diseased hands off of her, and get away." Penelopy then did something she had never, in all of her life, ever done, she got enraged! She raced by simple anger so quickly, no one even saw it pass. She disengaged from Marcus's arms, and approached her mother, her face red with her rage.

"Shut up!" she roared at Sophia. Her mother look at her, suddenly wide eyed at her daughters words, and attitude. Then she too lost her temper.

"You do not talk to me that way young lady!" she screamed back, and Penelopy got face to face with her mother.

"Shut Up!" she yelled again, even louder, and the surrounding people smiled, as did Marcus, as he looked to his future bride. The puffing Gordon and Xanaporia had arrived. The Sheriff looked like he would have been much happier anywhere else. Sophie, stunned to silence, stared at her daughter, with very wide eyes. "Marcus has asked me to marry him, and I have said yes, and, there is nothing you can do about it!" Penelopy yelled at her mother, and the anger returned to Sophia's eyes.

"Sheriff, arrest that pervert for trying to despoil my innocent daughter," she yelled, pointing at Marcus. She then looked at Penelopy. "You will marry the one I choose for you, not the offspring of a tinker!" she yelled at Penelopy. Again the group gasped, and Penelopy closed on her mother again. She was even madder than before.

"Mrs. Barnes," Gordon tried to intercede. "Giorgio Sordian was a paid up member of the Businessman's Association, and a well respected man in town." Sophia spun and glared at him.

"No one was talking to you, adulterer!" she yelled and turned back to Penelopy. That's when Xanaporia got mad.

"Maybe we should tell all, why your husband discharged the coachman," she yelled at Sophia. Sophia spun back around and stared at her. There were many chuckles heard, and nodding heads seen, by the crowd.

"That was an ugly rumor and a lie," Sophia squeaked. Xanaporia lifted one brow, and one side of her mouth.

"Was it really?" she asked very sarcastically, and loudly.

Mother!" Penelopy squawked. The volume and density of chuckles increased. Sophia spun back to her, trying to regain her composure, and the lead in this confrontation.

"It was an ugly lie, and there was never any disreputable behavior in our family," she stated, glancing at Gordon with a sneer. "Your father worked hard to give us the standing we have in this town, and I will not let you discredit that by marrying this mere tinkers son." Penelopy clouded up again.

"My father worked himself into an early grave to give you what your selfishness wanted," she spat at her mother. "And if you remember, his father, my grandfather, the one you would never let into our house, or anywhere near it, was a traveling peddler." The many chuckles now turned into laughter. Marcus came up and put his arm around Penelopy.

"You might as well face it, we're getting married," he told the glaring eyes of his future mother-in-law.

"Like hell you are," Sophia screamed. "Sheriff, my daughter is not old enough to be married without my consent, and I will not give it." The Sheriff looked to the suddenly smiling face of Penelopy.

"I turned sixteen a week ago," she stated, and looked to her mother. "You know, the birthday you forgot," she spat the last words at Sophia, whose eyes shot wide open. Penelope looked to the Sheriff; "You can check the court records," she told him, and turned back to her mother. "That means," Penelopy kept going; "that with Marcus being eighteen, and me sixteen, we are legally able to marry without your consent, and, we are going to!" Sophia clamped her jaws and leaned towards her.

"Fine, little miss stupid," she growled. "You are no longer my daughter, and you will not get anything from me but the clothes on your back." She turned, and started to walk away, as the slowly angering murmurs began among the gathered. She then stopped, and looked at the Sheriff. "I want all of those people out of my house!" she ordered him loudly. "God knows what they have stolen from me already." A gasp escaped the lips of the ever growing crowd.

"Ah, that is not possible Sophia," Gordon said calmly, as he and Xanaporia stepped closer to Sophia's glare. "Because of recent events, your house, like ours, and all others, has been commandeered for a shelter for all those who need one."

"If that is not to your satisfaction," Xanaporia said just as smoothly, a small smug, smile on her face; "perhaps, you, should find other quarters." Silence settled rapidly on everyone. The only sound was that of Sophia's rasping breath. Smiles began to reform on people's faces.

"Very well," Sophia's voice was threatening in tone. "I will, and the money of this town, will go with me." She spun and started to walk away.

"What do you mean?" Penelopy asked, her anger returning. "Have you kept money from all those who could use it, for what was needed?" She took a step towards her mother, her hands clenched in fists. Sophia stopped, and looked to her, with a horribly nasty smile. She then let her eyes travel over the crowd, returning to her disowned daughter.

"A lot more than simply money girl," she stated. "A lot more!" She turned, and continued on to her home, which was not very far away. Everyone exchanged looks for a few minutes, as Marcus again put his arms around Penelopy. She turned, and buried her face in his chest, weeping from her embarrassment of her mother, and her loss of her.

It was about six hours later, well after the lunch hour, that Dwayne Wilkman, the man it was rumored Sophia had been seeing in secret, was seen loading many strangely shaped crates, and large chests into a large, covered carriage, behind the house. Then he and Sophia were seen leaving town, in that same carriage, heading east. It was a few minutes after that, that the cry of fire was issued, and Sophia's house, very quickly, burnt to the ground.

Penelopy and Marcus were wed that very afternoon. Xanaporia acted as her bridesmaid, and Gordon, his best man. The entire town came together, shifting people so that the newlyweds could have Gordon and Xanaporia's bedroom, for their wedding night. It was learned, after the ruins of Sophia's house were explored, that Sophia had been hoarding money, jewels, art works, and gold, in a large hidden chamber, beneath her house.

Aaralyn, great granddaughter of Matsar and Drayson, and wife of Jarponer, was taking her turn on the talkers panel. Although one of the youngest on the panel, she was also one of the strongest talkers, and a very high magical power. She had already made several new connections, and was quite proud of what she had done. When the whining voice came to her, she responded as she had to the others' she had talked with. "Yes, what is your name, and the name of your domain?" she asked as she prepared to copy the names on the parchment before her.

"I am called Daridar, and I am from the domain called Bandarson," the voice told her, and Aaralyn raised her hand to signal she had made another new contact. Jennifer, the acting coordinator, came to her.

"What have you got?" she asked quietly, so as not do interrupt the connection. Aaralyn pointed to her writing.

"We are trying to find as many of the outer domains as we can, and warn them of a band of magical bandits,"

Aaralyn told Daridar. The Dwarf sat up, and Pestikar, assuming they were done, rose, and dressed, to follow Pinsikar's orders concerning the very fat, and very skinny Captains.

"What about them?" Daridar asked, as she watched her new mate dress, and then leave. Aaralyn was making notes on the parchment, and Jennifer read them as they were written.

"They attacked a town near a domain called the Plain, and we are trying to find out if anyone knows where their home world is," Aaralyn said, and Daridar smiled.

"Their home world is Bandarson," Daridar said, and all hell broke loose around the table of the talkers. Aaralyn didn't miss a beat.

"You say you are from Bandarson?" she asked casually. Daridar nodded to the empty room as she answered.

"Yes, and the one who lead the raid was called Porkligor, why?" she asked just as casually.

"Would you talk to us about it?" Aaralyn asked as more, and more, of the talkers tapped into her thoughts.

"I cannot," Daridar said as she rose from the bed, and slipped her simple gown over her head. "I have much work to do before my mate returns," she told the listeners, and broke the connection. Not a sound could be heard around the table of talkers, but their messages were traveling like lightning bolts, and loudly. Even someone with a limited ability to talk, heard them clearly.

When Isabella had been pulled into the bathing room, the first thing that Besaline had done was to put a necklace of some strange material around her neck, and a matching set of bracelets on her wrists. Then several female slaves, as naked as she, except that they had no body hair anywhere, pinned her hair up, and forced her into the water, and bathed her. They were neither gentle, nor shy, about what they cleaned. Isabella endured this assault on her body quietly. She was too involved in her own thoughts to worry about what these women did. She had been hearing the callings of the talkers, and she had been trying to answer, but they were not responding to her.

Brandaro walked into the bathing room just as Isabella was pulled from the water. She looked up into his amused eyes when he entered, and endured the examination his eyes gave her body. When he neared, his hands did the same to her. She neither shied from him, or acknowledged the actions of his hands on her. When he leaned around, and his hands settled on, and then kneaded her buttocks, Isabella saw the two women standing in the doorway with amused looks in their eyes, as they watched his hands work her body. She fought her blush, and did not succeed. The two women laughed at her. That is when Isabella heard Daridar's response. She fought her reaction, and Brandaro thought she was responding to his manipulations.

"My Lord," the larger of the two women said, as she too came into the room. "What are you to with this small one? If you try to enter her, she would split in two." Both women laughed again. Brandaro laughed as well, and released her.

"That is not why I want her Morselia," he said chuckling, and turned to Besaline. "I want her put into a full gown, and I want it to be red," he told her, and the slave master bowed. He turned back to Isabella, looking her over again. "Bring her to the throne room as soon as she has been readied," he added, and turned from her. Isabella saw the sudden look of hatred, that both of the women gave her, and she could feel the hatred behind those looks. As they left bathing room, Isabella looked down at her body, and saw that she now had no hair of any kind, except on her head. Her blush deepened. Besaline pointed to two other slaves, and they bowed, leaving the room, but quickly returned with a red garment between them.

"Raise your arms," Besaline command Isabella, and she complied. The two slid the gown down on her. It was much too big for her, but Besaline waved her hands, with a quick muttering, the gown fit her quite well. Tight on top, and looser down lower. Isabella didn't believe how much better she felt with her body covered. Her hair was then cruelly brushed, and tied in an elongated tail behind her. "Come," Besaline commanded, and Isabella followed her. She had listened to the conversation with Daridar, and she had become totally frustrated when Daridar, whoever she was, had broke the connection. She knew she had to find this Daridar, and soon!

"Alright, but where is this Bandarson?" Namson asked the large number of people who now filled the office, but there came no answer. He looked around at all that had answered his calling, and no one had a clue to give him.

"Aaralyn is still trying to reestablish contact, but as yet, there has been no reply," Jennifer told him, disappointment in her voice. Namson sighed, and nodded.

"I guess that is all we can do for now, but I want the other talkers to keep trying to make contacts. Maybe someone out there knows the location of this domain, and we can find it that way." Jennifer nodded, and left the room, returning to the panel of talkers who had already heard the Overseers words. Namson looked to Glornina, and nodded. She stood, and looked to all present.

"We have located the domain that is the second source of Amplifying stones, and where the bandits got theirs from," she announced. Phelilon, the representative sent by Perolon, from Elandif, looked up from the Power Stone that Glornina had brought back from Neponia, with worry in his eyes. The collected Keepers from each of the major domains nodded, and smiled to each other. This meeting included all three of Namson and Glornina's children. Glorian, their second, and her husband Braxton, from the Canyon, and Michele, their youngest, and her husband Crendoran, the new Ruler of Calisonnos. Zachia, the oldest, and his wife Emma, were sitting next to Glornina. Namson did not miss the look in the elves eyes.

"What is it Phelilon?" he asked, looking to the elf. Phelilon looked at him, and tried to smile.

"It is not something I am sure means anything, but this amulet is different from the one you have Overseer," Phelilon stated as he turned the amulet over in his hands.

"How so," Namson asked glancing at the amulet Phelilon worried with his hands. The elf looked to him, and then back to the stone.

"Well, first of all, and most confusing, is that there are twelve veins, instead of eight," the elf stated.

"What does that mean?" Namson asked quietly, after a glance at Glornina.

"I'm not sure Overseer. Perhaps nothing, and perhaps, a lot. I just don't know." Namson looked to the worried eyes of the elf, to the amulet, and back to the elf. "I would like Phemlon, and the elders, to look at it," Phelilon told him. "Perhaps they would better understand the meaning." Namson began to nod.

"Better understanding of what meaning?" Phemlon asked, entering the room. Phelilon looked to him, and held out the Amulet to him. Phemlon took it, and looked it over. Namson saw the sudden tension of Phemlon, and again glanced at Glornina. She too had seen the leader of elves of the Realm, tense, when he had looked at the Amulet. She shrugged slightly to her husband.

"What is it Phemlon?" Namson asked softly, so as not to distract the others' in the room, who were whispering among themselves. Phemlon took a slow deep breath, and then looked at Namson.

"I think that Phelilon is correct, that the elders should look at this," he said, coming closer to Namson. He extended the amulet to him. "In the mean time, perhaps you should keep this well guarded!" he added in a whisper. Namson reached for the amulet as he searched for meanings in Phemlon's eyes.

"Why?" Namson asked, whispering as well. Phemlon smiled, slightly.

"It could be only an old rumor, but the elders would know more about it than I," Phemlon told him, but Namson saw an intensity in the elves eyes. He nodded, and spelled the amulet to the same vault that held the one he had inherited from Mike. "I will contact the elders here in the Realm, and Perolon on Elandif. As soon as we can get it organized, I think we should bring them here, and let them view the amulet," Phemlon said in a more normal tone. Namson nodded again.

"Very well," he said in the same tone. "I will await your word that all is ready." Namson added a small grin to his words. He could see Glornina out of the corner of his eye, and he did not like the look of concern in her eyes, as she looked at him.

Chapter Three

Emma slowly, and gently, rubbed her slightly swollen abdomen as she talked with her two sisters-in-laws. The seven children played near them. The three oldest making sure their younger brothers, sisters, and cousins, were happy. Glorian's twins, both boys, and just crawling, would not leave Mike, Emma's oldest, at almost three, alone. Probably because he was the only other boy in the bunch. She was proud that Mike was showing patience with the babies. Heather, Glorian's oldest, at almost two, and Mearlanor, Michele's oldest, the same age as Heather, were both acting as little mother's. They had all met on the rear terrace of the palace, right after the meeting, and they were trying to figure out what it all meant. The three husbands and fathers, stood separate from them, but were constantly looking in their direction, to make sure all was calm.

"Has Zachia told you anything?" Glorian asked Emma as she snagged Telkor, one half of her set of twin boys, and checked his diaper. Emma shook her head, smiling at the actions of the boy, for this sudden intrusion of his play.

"Crendoran isn't telling me anything," Michele said, as she stopped her youngest daughter, Dafnorian, from seeing how far she could pull Merganía's, Emma's youngest, hair, before the girl cried.

"No," Emma said as she looked to her husband. "He has been in conference with his father a lot, but he isn't telling me much."

"You're pregnant again, aren't you?" Glorian asked as she looked to Emma's hand. Emma blushed, and nodded, with a growing smile. Michele grinned and nodded as well, not realizing who the question had been directed at. They all chuckled as she blushed as well.

———————

"What's going on Zachia?" Braxton asked. Crendoran nodded his desire to know as well. Zachia glanced at his wife, and children, and then looked back to Braxton.

"Have you or your father had any more sensing's of the bandits?" he asked quietly. Braxton, a very powerful sensitive himself, shook his head, as he looked to Zachia with a strange look.

"Not so much the bandits, but papa said he had a sensing one of the captured girls." Zachia and Crendoran both looked to him. "He doesn't know which one, but said he felt the presence from a spike of emotion, which means the girl has magical power."

"Has he told anyone, besides you I mean?" Crendoran asked. Braxton shrugged.

"He told Quansloe, but he said it was only a split second, and then nothing," Braxton told them.

"One of the girls has magical powers?" Zachia asked, more to himself. Braxton nodded.

"Quansloe, and my father, are in Zentler right now, trying to find out which one of the captured had any powers. If anyone knew about them that is."

"That's why Hannah's here with Xanadera," Zachia said. Braxton nodded as the wives' informed them that it was lunch time, and that they, and the children, were hungry. The three chuckled, and joined their families, as they all went into the palace. Zachia told himself to check later with his father, and see what he had learned.

———— ⋙ ⋘ ————

"I do not trust these new humans," Waltzorn stated as he and Wenzorn walked to the fitting room. That room was where the second to last stage was preformed with the Power Stones. There the Stones were placed into the amulets, and melded together.

"You said the same of Mistress Cartope, and her group Waltzorn," the leader of the Mearlies stated calmly. "Now you rave of their value to Neponia."

"Did you not hear of the power they possess? Did you not hear that the Queen is concerned about that power? Why would she then give one of our Power Stones to the female?" Waltzorn asked with more of an angry tone than Wenzorn thought proper. He turned to Waltzorn, and gave him his look. His second dropped his eyes. "I am sorry Wenzorn, but I truly feel danger in this alliance the Queen is forming."

"I understand Waltzorn, but we must trust our Queen," Wenzorn said softly, placing his large hand on his friends shoulder. "These humans you worry about, are in danger from the bandits as well. You heard the little ones premonition as well as I." Waltzorn nodded, and took a deep breath.

"If it is yours, and the Queens will," Waltzorn said resignedly, and turned to attend his duties. Wenzorn smiled after him, and turned to the approaching Line Chief.

"Chief Wezzorn, how goes the work?" he asked as the Chief stopped, giving the proper bow of respect. The Chief straightened, and grinned. He extended the work sheet to his ruler.

"We are at the proper production speed at every position Wenzorn," the Chief stated with pride. Wenzorn allowed a slight smile as he took the sheets, and looked over the figures written. His head nodded with approval as he finished the reading.

"Excellent Chief, congratulate all of your workers, and keep the proper time tables," Wenzorn said, and turned to go back to his office. As he walked, he thought. It takes two years to make one amulet properly, though the stones were manufactured hundreds at a time, and there were stones being worked in every stage, constantly. It is critical, at each stage of production, that the proper procedures, and timing, be maintained. His thoughts returned to the disaster that had happened in the Northern Section, and he shuddered at the destruction, and loss of life, both Mearlie, and human. It had all happened because the Mearlie ruler had decided to take short cuts in time and procedures. Then to have that chest of questionable amulets stolen by the bandits not six weeks later. He shuddered as he thought of what might happen if someone with a strong magical power were to try to use those amulets, seeking an even more powerful result.

<hr />

Gremble, the leader of the Realm ogres, and his mate Grandoa, who had kept their rooms at the palace after Morgan's death, at the insistence of Mike, and that had been continued with Namson, entered the gate as they returned to the palace from a visit with their daughter, and grandchildren. "Grable and Minstoa are good parents," Gremble stated softly, for an ogre. Grandoa chuckled.

"I cannot believe how much Meathoa has grown, and, that Grimtal is going to be difficult when he gets bigger!" she said, and her chuckle turned to a laugh. "And at the rate he's growing, that will not be long!" Gremble joined in her laughter, as they thought of the newest member to the family, who barely walking, was already getting into everything his parents could not stop him from, and that was more than they wanted to admit!

"Gremble!" a booming voice called from behind them. They both turned, recognizing the voice of their old friend Mursel, the retired clan leader of the trolls of the Plain. They were surprised to see not only Mursel, but his mate Cailson, Coursel, the son of Mursel and the current clan leader, and his mate Censon. Worsel, the retired clan leader of the trolls of the Valley and his mate Morson, and Morsel, son of Worsel, and current Valley clan leader, and his mate Quenson as well, exiting a portal. They were joined by the trolls of the Realm, Zardan and his mate Bilson, Ponsel, and his mate Heathson, Porsel and his mate Daison, as they walked up to the gate. Greetings were made as friends met, the females separating from the males, as was their custom. Both Gremble and Grandoa had gone down to one knee, so that their friends didn't have to be looking up that high.

"There you are Gremble!" a small voice called out, and they all looked up to see the faxlie Tremliteen, coming lower. "I was to go to the home of Grable and Minstoa, to tell you that the Overseer would like you to join in the meeting he has asked for, with the trolls."

"Well, we have saved you a trip then," Gremble told the smiling faxlie. Tremliteen shook his head without losing his smile.

"I am returning," he said with a laugh. The others joined him. Gremble looked to Mursel, saddened by the signs of age on his friend.

"Do you know what this meeting is for?" he asked. The troll shrugged, and they all laughed again. "Well then, we should not keep the Overseer waiting. Let us find out." He rose, and helped Grandoa to her feet. Together, the group marched into the palace. Pelkraen, the lead Meleret of the palace, met them, and immediately led them to the smaller meeting room, where Namson and Tarson awaited them. The joyful mood of all was squelched, when they saw the looks on their faces. They all quickly found seats, and waited for Namson to speak.

"You have all heard of the raid on Zentler," Namson finally said, and they all nodded.

"Is it true the bandits have Amplifying Stooooones?" Coursel asked. Namson nodded.

"But, there is more to it," he added. "The stones they have are different than the ones we have used." The trolls and ogres exchanged confused looks. "We don't know yet what that means, but I think it wise to prepare for the worst, and be happy if it turns out the other." There were nods throughout. "Gremble, I am asking that you have the ogres, work closely with Tarson, and the Army of the Realm." The ogre nodded, with a glance at Tarson. Namson looked to the trolls. "Are there still plenty of Milky Quartz?" he asked. Every troll smiled, and nodded. "Good," Namson said. "I'm asking that you work with the elves, and be ready for the making of shields in the sizes we may need, at a moment's notice," Namson asked, and they all again nodded. "As I said, we don't know for sure what we're up against yet, but I want us all to be ready for anything that comes." Mursel had been staring at Namson, and it was obvious that he was in deep thought.

"Ooooverseer, you say these bandits have magical poooowers?" Mursel asked, and Namson nodded. "Is it poooossible that these bandits might knoooow oooof oooour Milky Quartz?" he asked solemnly. Namson now returned his stare, as his right brow rose. He then slowly smiled.

"I had not thought of that possibility Mursel, but now that you have, I think we can make ourselves ready in case they do know, and decide they want some!" Mursel and the others joined in his grin, and added their nods. "I will contact Quansloe, and see what we can do." Namson added. There were nods, and smiles of agreement, by all.

Long before she came to the doorway, Isabella heard the cries, and moans, of the other eight girls who had been taken from Zentler with her. She did not have to think too hard to realize what was happening to them. Tears fought to come to her eyes. When she did reach the door, she could not stop herself from looking. The girls hands were tied to the center post of a round bed. They were naked, and they were being raped, as other men stood around, waiting their turn. She could easily see that several of the girls were bleeding from their assaults. She tore her eyes from the scene, knowing it was only a matter time before she too, would face the same fate. She battled her tears, and lifted her head, as Besaline stopped in front of a huge door, guarded by two very large men. They swung the door open, and Besaline lead her into the room. She followed Besaline with her head held high. She saw the huge man, and the two women, sitting on an extravagant couch. She saw the he had removed his shirt, and Isabella almost gasped out loud, at the size of his upper body, but the medallion he wore around his neck was what caught her eyes, and it reminded her of something, but she couldn't think of what. The two women glared at her, and the man smiled, when she was stopped in front of the three.

"Show the proper respect to your master!" Besaline stated, and nudged her. The slave master would have normally cuffed this little one a good one, but she knew the meaning of the red gown, and only dared a nudge. Isabella refused, and stared steadily into the man's eyes, her head still held high.

"That's enough Besaline, leave us," Brandaro said calmly. The two women looked to him, their anger clear in their eyes. He ignored them as he looked at Isabella. The sounds of the abused girls cries had been cut off when the door had been closed behind her, but with Besaline's leaving, and doors opening to let her out, Isabella again heard the horrible sounds. Her rage was not withheld from her eyes as she looked to the man. He chuckled, knowing what angered her. "That is now the only value they have to me. To keep my male slaves satisfied!" He let a snarl come to his lips, as he looked back into her eyes. Her intensity of anger amused him. He smiled as he spoke. "Do you know why you are not in that room as well?" he asked her calmly. She didn't trust her voice, so she slowly shook her head. "You have magical power, and you were taken from a place that should not have had any like you," he told her simply. Morselia and Caratelia looked to him, and then her, with surprised looks. Isabella suddenly felt a chill start up her back. He leaned forward, his look of amusement, changed to angry intensity. "Now, tell me about the Realm, the Plain, and what you know of the stones that can absorb cast spells!" She could not stop the flicker from her eyes, as the chill turned to fear.

In the Mayor's office, Quansloe and Mentalon, stared at Gordon and Xanaporia. They were so surprised by what they had been told, they couldn't even widen their eyes.

"Are you sure of this?" Quansloe finally asked, and Gordon nodded, as Xanaporia looked to her husband.

"Yes," Gordon told them. "I am very sure. I know this, because she is my daughter." This time the two did open their eyes in surprise, and they both looked to Xanaporia.

"She is his daughter, from a different woman," she told them softly as she took Gordon's hand in both of hers. "An indiscretion that he has paid full price for," she added. Gordon dropped his eyes with her words.

"And she is a strong magical talent?" Quansloe asked quietly. Both Gordon and Xanaporia nodded, as Gordon lifted his eyes.

"A very powerful magical talent, that does not need a source," he told them. Quansloe and Mentalon looked to each other.

"They must have discovered her power, and shielded her abilities," Mentalon said, and Quansloe nodded. "That would explain the sudden ceasing of my sensing of her." Again Quansloe nodded, as they both turned back to Gordon. It was Xanaporia who stopped their questions.

"If it is possible, she will find a way to contact us," she told them. "She is a very resourceful young woman." All three men looked to her. Two with hope, and a Mayor, with surprise.

⌐⌐⌐⌐⌐⌐⌐⌐⌐⌐⌐

Across town from the mayor's office, and the surprise of Quansloe and Mentalon, Penelopy kissed Marcus, and turned to enter the kitchens. She was helping prepare the meals the entire population of Zentler shared. Marcus had a purpose of his own, and that was one Melsikan. He and Penelopy had found time to talk on their wedding night, despite their hunger of each other. Penelopy had told him of Isabella's powers, as well as her joining with Melsikan, in love, and pleasure. He found his quarry helping with the demolition of one of the burnt houses.

"Melsikan, may I talk with you?" Marcus called to him. Melsikan looked to him as he straightened from stacking boards, to be carried. His eyes stayed on Marcus for several seconds before he stopped what he was doing, and started towards the new groom. He pulled the leather gloves from his hands as he walked through the debris, his eyes steadily staring into Marcus's. Marcus began to feel uneasy under the steady stare.

"What do you want?" Melsikan asked, stopping before him. Marcus tried to smile.

"I think we need to talk," he said. He could easily see the still evident bruises from the beating Melsikan had taken, the night of the raid.

"About what?" Melsikan asked, his posture at ease, but his eyes intensifying.

"Isabella," Marcus said softly, returning Melsikan's stare evenly. It was few seconds before Melsikan gave a small nod, and led him to a remote area, away from listeners. Melsikan finally stopped, and turned to Marcus.

"What about her?" he asked, his eyes still intense, but the badly hidden pain of her loss, showed as well.

"Were you aware she has magical powers?" Marcus didn't hesitate in his directness, and was completely unprepared for Melsikan's decided lack of a surprise, in his reaction.

"Yes, what about it?" he answered, with a slight nod. It was Marcus's turn to hesitate before answering.

"How could they take her, if she had magical abilities?" he finally asked. Melsikan sighed as he looked to the others still working, and then back to Marcus.

"How much do you know of magic?" he asked calmly, and quietly. Marcus smiled before he answered.

"Very little, I have to admit," he said. "Penelopy just told me last night of Isabella's abilities, and about other things. Though it did explain some things I have seen, and didn't understand. I'm not real sure I understand, or even believe all she told me, but you obviously do, so why didn't she stop what was happening?" Melsikan sighed again.

"What did she tell you?" Melsikan asked, his voice not changing in tone or volume. Marcus thought for a moment.

"About Isabella's powers. Places called the Valley, and Plain, and someplace called the Realm," Marcus told him, and Melsikan nodded. Marcus's eyes opened slightly as he realized that Melsikan seemed to know of these places. Melsikan took his arm, and led him farther from any that could overhear them.

"Isabella is a very powerful magical talent," he told Marcus as they started to walk. "She was defeated, and taken, because of the amulets the raiders wore." They stopped in the morning shade of one of the few trees in town that had survived. Not only out of earshot, but out of sight of the other workers. Marcus looked at him in confusion. Melsikan did not smile as he spoke.

"They were wearing Amplifying Stones, and they could overpower whatever spell she cast at them." Marcus looked more confused. Melsikan went on to explain of the battles with the Dark Magic forces, the Valley, Plain, and the Realm. He told the wide eyed Marcus of the old and new Overseer of the Realm. He told of all the races, and domains. It was nearing lunch time when he finished his telling. Marcus had stood quietly, never interrupting. At times his eyes wide, and other times angered, and yet other times, near to tears. When Melsikan finished, and was again quiet, looking into Marcus's eyes, Marcus could only ask one question.

"How do you know all of this?" he whispered the question. Marcus did not think that any further telling could surprise him more, but when Melsikan told of his own past, and powers, he discovered that he could be!

It was shortly after lunch that Phemlon told Namson, that Telalon was ready. Namson nodded, and the elder elf appeared in his office, his arms supported by his two younger, but not young, aides. Namson and Glornina bowed with respect to the old one. He responded with more ability than they thought he would possess. Namson indicated the large, well cushioned chair that had been placed in front of his desk, and the two aides helped Telalon to sit.

"Telalon," Namson started, as both he and the elf, sat. Glornina stood beside him, her right hand resting on his left shoulder. Phemlon took position at the end of the desk. "We thank you for your acceptance of our invitation, and your efforts to come." He finished with a slight bow to the elder. Again Telalon nodded his recognition of the Overseer's honoring.

"Phemlon has told me of the stone," Telalon said, getting directly to the point. "May I see it please?" Namson nodded, and spelled the amulet to himself. One of the aids passed it to Telalon. The old elf took a quick look at it, and without lifting his head, his eyes looked to Namson. "May I see the stone you possess?" he asked quietly. Namson again nodded, and spelled the Amplifying Stone he had received from Mike, to himself, and the aid passed it to Telalon. The old elf sighed, and looked to the Overseer. "Come, I must show you this," he told Namson. Namson and Glornina, came to the chair, one to each side. "Here," Telalon said, as he pointed to four of the eight veins, one at a time. "You see these veins?" Namson and Glornina nodded. "If you were to look at the stone as a compass, the four larger veins point north, south, east, and west." Telalon's thin finger pointed out the thicker, four curved veins that ran from the red core.

"I see what you say," Namson said, noticing for the first time that the four indicated veins were indeed thicker, though not by much, than the other four.

"The other four veins," Telalon pointed to the other four that were positioned between the four thicker ones; "give support the primary ones. Covering every direction around the core, which is where the power is located." The withered elf placed the amulet in his lap, and picked up the one Glornina had brought from Neponia. Namson immediately saw what the elder was getting at. There were two thinner veins between the primary ones.

"This one is a greater amplifier," Namson's whispered words were heard by all, as he looked into the eyes of the elder elf. Telalon nodded slowly.

"The original stone would amplify greatly, but this one," Telalon lifted the amulet higher as they all looked to it; "would do so twice the first!" A deathly silence followed his words, as they all realized what his words truly meant. "I would truly like to meet the ones who made this amulet," Telalon said softly, lowering the amulet until he again held it with both hands. Namson looked to Glornina. She nodded, and called to Cartope. Minutes passed, and no one, especially Namson, liked the look that came to her face. She finally nodded, and looked to Namson.

"Cartope says that Neponities will not allow the Mearlies to leave Neponia." Glornina did not try to hide her anger, as Telalon looked to her with surprise in his eyes. "We will have to travel there to meet with them. She also said that the Queen will allow only you and I, with Telalon and his two aides, to come." Namson nodded, glancing at the quickly recovering elf elder.

"Have her set a time for our arrival," he told her. She concentrated as Telalon looked back and forth between them. His face showing his growing excitement. More minutes passed, and finally, Glornina looked to her husband.

"She says later this afternoon. She will send a picture of where we are to arrive," she said. Namson nodded as he began to let his thoughts take him.

———————

Daridar, very angry that Pestikar had come home, only to use her quickly, thinking only of his own pleasures, and had then left, telling her that he would not be home until very late. She finally remembered the voice she had spoken to before. "Are you still there?" she called out with her thoughts.

"Yes Daridar," the voice told her with surprise, though it seemed a different tone than the one before. "We are still here. We are very happy that you called. Can we talk of your home world now?" the voice asked. Alexania was frantically waving her hands to alert all that she had regained connection with the voice from Bandarson. The rest tapped into her mind as Daridar, still angry at her new mate, replied.

"Why are males only interested in their own pleasures?" she all but yelled at the listening minds. Most of the talkers were female, and they all turned and looked at the three males on the panel. The poor innocent men shrugged.

"What do you . . . ?" Alexania tried to ask.

"He comes in here, uses me as a common parsha, and then tells me he will be gone the day long. What about what I want?" Daridar did yell that. "I don't like that!"

she yelled again, and her anger caused her to break the connection. There were wide eyes around the table, but they quickly turned to glares, as they all turned, and stared at the poor three men who had no idea what they had done. Daridar stewed in her anger for awhile, and then thoughts began to come to her. She began to smile as they did.

Cartile soared with the wind, as he looked over the land. Jastile had gone to visit with their daughter, Semitile, and her mate, Merlintile, and his grandchildren, and great grandchildren. He smiled as he saw the farmers working the fields, and the cattle that looked up at him, and then went back to their grass. He found a good thermal, and it lifted him higher. He let himself be lost in the simple pleasure of flight. When he swung back towards the City Realm, he saw the Realm armies practicing in the large field behind the Elder of the Guardians residence. His happy mood was lost, as he thought that again, they must fight against those who would try to take without right. He lowered, and could make out Crastamor as he led the dragons in aerial practice at low level. The Black Dragon had become more than a friend, since his son, Merlintile, had paired with Cartile's daughter. Cartile lowered even more to learn what was being planned. Crastamor saw him land, and called for a break in the dragons training, which was a relief to more than one. Crastamor landed near the Leader of the Realm dragons.

"Cartile, it is good to see you my friend," Crastamor told him as he walked near. Cartile nodded, and smiled to his friend.

"I have come to learn what preparations are being made," he told the Black Dragon as they stopped, facing each other, though Cartile had to look up slightly, to the larger Black Dragon. Crastamor nodded. He looked around, and then back to Cartile.

"All is going well," he said. "We are training to battle ground forces, as Tarson, and the Overseer, do not yet think that there will be an aerial force to face," Crastamor told him. "But, there is a rumor that they do possess Amplifying Stones, and we are trying to learn what defenses the Overseer has planned against that." Again Cartile nodded as he looked around at the training forces.

"I do not see Merlintile?" Cartile said softly, and Crastamor shook his head.

"He is at the palace," Crastamor told him. "The Overseer called for him, Semitile, Zaclitile, and Maratile, early this morning," he added, speaking of both of their children, and grand children. Cartile looked to him with confusion, wondering of his mates location.

"Why would the Overseer call for them?" he wondered out loud, and Crastamor did a dragons shrug. "Perhaps I should find out," Cartile said with a smile; "before I go making assumptions." Again Crastamor shrugged, this time with a nod, and a smile. "Until later my friend," Cartile said and leapt into the air, turning towards the

Overseers palace, to find out the Overseers plans for his daughter, son-in-law, grandson and his mate. He had barely gotten height when he saw the four in question, as well as Jastile, lift from the palace, and come towards him. They all met as they turned towards the western mountains. Cartile did not like the serious expressions he saw on their faces. They landed in the large pasture in front of the cliffs that held the caves that were their homes.

"What has the Overseer asked of you?" Cartile asked Merlintile, as Jastile moved to his side. The mostly black, and larger than any dragon in the Realm, including his father, looked to him, and he was worried.

"The Amplifying Stones used by the bandits are twice the power of the ones we have had," Merlintile told him quietly. Cartile looked to his grandson and his mate, and they nodded their conformation. Jastile looked to Cartile.

"What are we to do?" she asked her mate quietly. He smiled to her, and gently nuzzled her neck.

"Whatever we must my love, whatever we must," he told her, his eyes traveling from one of the younger dragons, to the next. Merlintile, the strongest in magical power of all dragons, though Semitile, and their children, were very close to his powers, nodded slightly, his jaws clenched.

"I don't know what you are talking about." Isabella's voice sounded much more firm than she had expected it to. Brandaro's backhand struck faster than Isabella could see. He had done it softly, by his standards, but Isabella's head snapped around, and she flew a distance, from the impact. She pulled herself from the floor without touching the jaw she knew must be broken. She got back up, and walked back until she again faced the angry Brandaro. She looked to his eyes, trying to ignore the pain. Her anger still demonstrated in her stare, as blood eased from her split lip. She waited, afraid to try and move her jaw, to speak. He pulled his hand back again, and she did not flinch, keeping a constant eye contact with him. From the corner of her sight, she saw the two women lean forward, smiling. Waiting for the second slap to send her flying again. Suddenly Brandaro smiled, and lowered his hand. Isabella sighed, in her mind.

"You are strong indeed," he told her as he settled back on the couch. The two women looked to him with surprise, and anger. "I will give you some time to think of the options that face you if you fail to obey again," he told her, letting his eyes travel over her, as he beckoned to a guard nearby. The guard stopped next to Isabella, and came to attention.

"Yes Lord Brandaro," the guard stated loudly. Brandaro never took his eyes from Isabella.

"Put her in the cell off from my quarters," he told the guard.

"Yes Lord Brandaro," the guard replied. He pulled a short sword from its scabbard, and faced her. "Come," he commanded Isabella. She obeyed, and went with him. She silently thank everything, when she was led out a different door than the one she had entered. She did not think she could bear hearing the cries of the abused girls again. The guard led her through several different corridors as she slowly tried working her jaw. She was pleasantly surprised to find it respond, with only a little pain.

The guard stopped in front a wooden door, and replaced his sword in its scabbard. He pulled a large key from his vest pocket, and opened the cell door. "In," he ordered. Isabella entered the dark, and dank room. The door shut behind her, followed by the sounds of the lock being engaged. She looked around the room, lit only by the small window in the door. She saw a flat wooden bed, with another thick piece of wood that was obviously supposed to be a pillow. In one corner she saw a pot, and knew that was the only comfort she was to have. She crossed to the bed, and sat down. She started to reach for the hem of the dress she wore, to wipe the blood from her mouth, when the dim light was reduced even more. She looked to the door, and saw the leering face of the guard looking at her. She remembered her nakedness, and let go of the hem of the dress, and glared back at the beast in the window. He laughed, and turned away. She heard his steps as he returned to his duties. She waited, to see if any others were going to spy on her. After several minutes, she guessed there was to be no one else, for a while anyway, and used the hem to wipe the blood from her mouth, very gently. When satisfied she could get no more cleaned from her sore mouth, she lay back on the bed, placing her head on the wooden block that was her pillow. Her thoughts raced. She tried not to think of the poor girls suffering in that distant room. She didn't know, until much later, that only a few survived the first raping, and those who had, did not live much longer, for the other cruelties done to them.

"What have I seen that can help me get to this Daridar?" she asked herself in a whisper.

"Why would you want to get to something like Daridar?" a hushed voice asked from a darkened corner. "She is nothing but a dwarf." Isabella had seen no other person in the room when she had entered. She pulled her head up, and looked to the corner the voice had come from. A shadow turned into a young girl, as she came from the corner. Isabella looked at her with surprise.

"There was no one in this room when I entered," she whispered, with a glance at the doors window. "How did you get in here?" The girl smiled.

"I have my ways," she said simply. "Why would you seek Daridar, a dwarf of no importance. Don't you know that all dwarves will turn on their own kind if there is a profit to it?" she asked again. Isabella quickly looked the girl over. She looked around ten or eleven years old. Her clothes hiding any sign of growing maturity, but Isabella had to admit that those clothes would have hidden her shape as well.

"Who are you?" Isabella asked, with another glance to the door.

"I am called Kris, by any that would admit to knowing me," the girl answered calmly, but a grin had come to the corners of her mouth. Isabella could not but feel that there could not be many who would admit to knowing this girl.

"Do you know Daridar?" Isabella asked as she sat up. The girl pulled back from her.

"Lay back down!" she hissed. Isabella immediately lay down. She looked to the girl, and saw that she had moved to the door, and was listening intently. Isabella had never heard the girl move. Finally, Kris nodded slightly, and returned silently to the foot of the bed. "I know of her. She is the newly bid mate of Pestikar, a spy for Pinsikar."

"Can you take me to her?" Isabella asked. "It is very important!" Her whisper turning intense. Kris looked into her eyes for a moment, and then traveled the length of her.

"You must be very important to Brandaro," she whispered, allowing a sly grin to appear. "A full red gown, and he has not let any of his men have you yet. Plus, he only slapped you gently." Isabella looked at her, surprised again. "What's in it for me if I do?" the girl asked.

"Freedom from the cruelty of him, and to be able to walk freely, without fear of what Brandaro's men might do to you," Isabella whispered, lifting her head more. "Freedom for all the peoples of this place!" The girl covered her mouth to quiet her laughter. She finally looked to Isabella, a wide grin on her face.

"No one wants freedom here, especially the males." She sneered through her grin. "Why would they? They have all the women to use as they please, and all the monies they want, though their greed constantly drives them to want more! Why would they want, or allow, freedom of any kind?" Isabella felt sorrow for the truth of the girls words.

"What of the women?" she asked, lifting her head even higher. "Do they feel pleasure from the abuse they receive?" Isabella's voice got slightly louder. "Do you want that when you are physically ready? That a man could, and would, just take you as he pleases?" A harsh, sneering smile came to the girls face.

"I am already physically ready, and there will be no man, *just taking*, me for his pleasure," she told Isabella, her voice had turned as hard as her smile. "I can guarantee that!"

"What's to stop them?" Isabella hissed at her, and the sounds of footsteps came to them both. Isabella looked to the door, and then back to the girl, but Kris was not there. "Kris?" Isabella called quietly. She had just returned her head to the block of wood when Brandaro's face appeared in the window of the door.

"I will let you think on the possibilities of your future, overnight," he told her. "I think you will see the advantage of cooperation when you are brought to me tomorrow, naked!" Isabella stared at the ceiling as the sound of the two women's laughter came to her. She hoped that they could not see the trembling that had come to her.

—————

Namson, Glornina, Telalon, and his two aides, appeared in front of a very plain wooden building, at the base of a very large mountain. Glornina had warned them all of the mode of dress the Neponian's maintained, so Namson, nor the elves, were shocked by the virtually nude people who walked from the building. Neponities, Traredonar, Cartope, and Ralsanac, stopped, and then bowed to the visitors. Namson, and the others returned the bows. Glornina took a short step forward.

"Overseer, may I present Neponities, Queen of the Central Section of Neponia." Her hand indicated the tall lithe woman, who stood in front of the others. The Queen bowed, and Namson returned the bow, making sure his eyes stayed with hers. She felt no such compunction, and her eyes traveled over him. There seemed a pleased expression in them. This was not missed by Glornina. "Her Chosen Mate Traredonar," Glornina said quickly. The man bowed and Namson returned it. "Cartope, and her Chosen Mate Ralsanac," Glornina added, and the two gave their bows. Glornina did not like the look in Cartope's eyes as she too looked her husband over. "Everyone," even Glornina heard the irritation in her own voice; "the Overseer of the Realm, Namson, my husband!" The last word had an emphasis on it. "Telalon, of Elandif, and his two assistants." She finished the introductions, not missing the amused looks of Neponities, and Cartope.

"Welcome to Neponia, Overseer of the Realm," Neponities said with a calm, regal voice. Namson again bowed slightly, fighting the smile caused by his wife's tone of voice. "There is much, I feel we should discuss, later."

"It could be that you are right Your Majesty, and please, call me Namson," Namson replied. Neponities smiled, and looked to Telalon. Her eyes quickly scanned him, head to toe, and back.

"You bear a striking resemblance to the Mearlies, though you are much taller," she told him. Telalon smiled, and nodded.

"I mean no disrespect Your Majesty, but may we meet these Mearlies? At my age, it is not wise to delay anything too long." Telalon was smiling with his words, and Neponities joined his smile.

"Your races even share a directness to your words. Please, follow me," she said, and turned back to the door they had emerged from. Cartope walked with her, as the two men stepped out of the way, to allow the visitors entry. Namson and Glornina followed the Queen and Cartope, with Telalon and his aides following them. When they entered the surprising large interior of the building, the first thing that impressed Namson, besides the very nice, exposed figures of the Queen and Cartope, was the simplicity of the settings. The long, slightly curved couch, facing two much smaller straight couches, with a table at two different levels between, were all the furnishings in the large room. Off to the left, there was what looked to be a small kitchen area, with a counter in front. It was to there that the two men went, as the women led them to the large couch. The Queen sat at the far end of the couch, indicating that Telalon should sit on the other end. She then smiled at Namson, and indicated the place next to her. Namson smiled, and sat. Cartope then cut Glornina off, and sat down next to him. Glornina fought her anger as she sat between Cartope and Telalon. Namson did not miss Cartope's move, or the look in his wife's eyes. He was quite sure he was going to hear all about it later.

"Namson," Cartope started, in a tone of voice that did absolutely nothing to calm Glornina's irritation. Namson turned to her, looking at her eyes, but his sight was on his wife. "Glornina has told us that there is none more powerful in magic than you. Is that true?" Her voice dripped with her unspoken desire. Glornina came very close to reaching out, and jerking two abundant handfuls of hair from her head. Namson did not miss his wife's reaction. He let his look go bland.

"That is correct," he told Cartope, looking directly into her eyes, and there was no doubt he meant it. "And I can assure you, that if anyone would know that, it would be my lovely wife," he added, and he saw a small smile tug at the corners of Glornina's mouth, as a rather shocked expression came to Cartope's eyes.

"Lord Overseer," Neponities stated, and asked, taking the attention from Cartope's rather blunt attempt. Namson turned to her, and he let a slight grin to come to his lips. "Very shortly, Wenzorn, leader of the Mearlies, his mate Yonlince, and the rest, shall be arriving." Namson nodded his understanding. "I should tell you that there are several in the Mearlies world, who are not happy of your presence, or the fact that I gave one of our Power Stones to Glornina." Again Namson nodded, not allowing his concerns to show. She looked back and forth between Namson and Telalon, as she continued. "As I said to Telalon, they can at times, be very direct in their words." When the Queen looked to him, Namson could not miss the slight look of worry that haunted her eyes. Namson smiled gently

"Wait until you meet a troll, or an ogre, Neponities," he said, and her eyes became confused, and Namson heard Glornina chuckle softly. "You have no need of concern. I am quite used to direct words. I actually find them preferable, for there are no hidden agendas, or any doubt of their meanings," he told the Queen, and he saw her relax. It was then that from a small doorway, near the far corner in the back of the building, a short being entered. Those of the Realm, and Elandif, raised their brows, for it looked exactly like an elf, except that its hands were out of proportion with its short body. They were much too big. Namson estimated the creature to be about three foot tall.

"Lord Wenzorn comes!" the messenger announced. The Queen rose, and all but Telalon, stood as well. Within seconds, a parade of the small beings came into the room. Six came to the two smaller couches, and the rest lined up behind the couches, and two stood guard at the door they had come through. The Mearlies bowed to the Queen, who returned it.

"Lord Wenzorn, allow me to present the Overseer of the Realm," Neponities said, indicating Namson with her hand. One male, in front of the couch, took a step forward, and gave a bow, though he never took his eyes from Namson's. Namson responded with the same eye contact. The Mearlie seemed impressed with his actions. "His mate Glornina." The Queen pointed to Glornina, and she bowed, quickly noticing that he did not want her eye contact in the bow. She dutifully lowered her eyes. He responded with a quick bow, and a interested look. "And this," Neponities said, pointing to Telalon. "Is Telalon, the representative from Elandif, the Elfin Domain." Wenzorn turned to the elf, and quickly lifted his hand to the efforts of Telalon to rise from the couch.

"I am very happy to finally be reunited with our distant cousins," he told Telalon, with a small bow, and a grin. The other Mearlies looked to their ruler with surprise, and then to the gentle smile on the much larger, elf's face.

"There are not many left who still know of the legend we share Wenzorn," he said softly with a small nod, and a smile. Wenzorn nodded.

"Perhaps it is time to familiarize them again with the tale?" he suggested with a wider grin. Telalon nodded as the Mearlies sat. All in the room were looking from one, to the other, as Wenzorn and Telalon had talked. Only Namson looked with the beginnings of an understanding. Once the Mearlies were seated, Neponities led the others, as they too sat.

"With your permission your Majesty," Namson stated, and the Queen nodded, once, slowly. "Telalon, perhaps you should lead the first part of this discussion." The elf looked to him with a nod, and a smile. When he looked to Wenzorn, there was a sadness in his eyes.

"There have been many, many, centuries since the great war." Telalon said, with same sadness his eyes had shown, as Namson and Glornina, as well as all the Neponian's looked to him in surprise.

"There was no greatness to it," Wenzorn said softly. "Both our races suffered from the arrogance of but a few." Telalon nodded his agreement.

"Perhaps it is time that foolishness is forgotten, and the truth be lived," Telalon suggested softly. Wenzorn nodded his agreement as another grin found his face, but it didn't last long.

"But this moment is not for the talk of that" he said, and looked to Namson. "You worry of the amulets the bandits possess," he said, and Namson nodded. Wenzorn looked at him for a moment, and then spoke, calmly, yet with force. "The amulets taken, were the results of a greedy Queen, and a stupid Mearlie Ruler!" Namson and Glornina glanced at Neponities and saw her head down. Namson returned his eyes to the Mearlie and saw anger where, calmness had been. "Because one human female thought she was due what she could not cope with, and the greed, and stupidity, of a Ruler who would not have been able to deal with what he had been promised, short cuts were taken in the making of the Power Stones! It cost many human, and Mearlie lives!" Namson watched the Rulers eyes, and saw no lessening of his anger, but then he saw fear creep into them as well. "The stones, that are dangerous because of the short cuts taken, were boxed together, and the Queen, who had survived the blast, stored them in her castle. In a few weeks, bandits attacked, killing, and stealing many for slaves, including the Queen, and the Stones!" Glornina and Cartope both watched Neponities, and they saw her nod slightly to the Mearlies words. Wenzorn's words became spaced, and almost guttural. "If the ones using those stones, are weak in their magical powers, or even a little higher, the stones will give them great powers!" Namson did not flinch from the stare of Wenzorn. "But if one with strong powers uses the stones, I fear what will happen, for the stones are unstable." Namson waited for more, but Wenzorn stayed quiet. Namson looked to Telalon, and saw that the elf was looking at him, with worry. He returned his eyes to Wenzorn.

"What would happen if one with a great power used the stones?" he asked softly. The Mearlie ruler looked at him for several moments, and then shrugged.

"I am not sure exactly, but I would not want to be anywhere in that domain, when they did," he said, just as softly. Namson heard Glornina's soft gasp.

"Mayor!" Marcus called out. Gordon turned, and saw the young man pulling the storekeeper Melsikan, with him. Penelopy walked with them, and she was grinning quite widely. As they neared, Gordon remembered that Isabella had told him of her love for the storekeeper. His heart went out to the young man.

Immediately after Melsikan had explained his history, and powers, Marcus had all but dragged him to the kitchens. He had gotten Penelopy out of the kitchen, and had Melsikan tell her what he had told him. She had become quite excited, and told them both that they needed to talk with the mayor. She told them both that Melsikan must get to the Overseer as soon as possible! "Mayor," Penelopy said as they stopped in front of him; "we need to talk with you, in private!" Gordon looked at her with surprise, for the intensity of her voice.

"Why, what can be so . . . . ?"

"Isabella has told me of her special, abilities," Penelopy said, her voice was hushed, but still very intense. Gordon looked to her for a moment, and then around the town.

"Come, we're not far from my office. We can talk there," he told them as he glanced at Melsikan. The look in the young man's eyes, told him that they all knew about his daughters talents. The four walked quickly to the mayor's office. When they arrived, Gordon closed the door behind the other three as they settled in chairs. Penelope kept glancing at Melsikan. Gordon settled into his chair behind his desk, and looked, one by one, to the three before him.

"All right, what's so important?" he asked calmly, clasping his hands, and leaning forward, placed his clasped hands, and forearms, on his desk. Both Penelopy and Marcus looked to Melsikan.

"Tell him," Penelopy begged. Gordon looked to her, and then to the young man before him. Melsikan's head was down, refusing to meet the mayor's eyes. "Tell him!" Penelopy yelled at him, and Melsikan was not the only one to jump from the volume of her yell. He glared at her, and them looked to the mayor, his face and eyes turning calm.

"How much do you know of Mike's quest to learn of Maltakrine?" he asked calmly, and Gordon's eyes began to open wide. He stared into the eyes of Melsikan.

"How much do you know?" he asked very quietly. Melsikan smiled.

"I asked you first," he told the mayor, and both Marcus and Penelopy chuckled. Gordon looked to them, and then back to Melsikan.

"Oh shit," he whisper, as he spun his chair completely around, and opened a lower cabinet behind him. He pulled an orb from the cabinet, and placed it on his desk. The wide eyes of Marcus and Penelopy, and the calm, knowing eyes of Melsikan, watched as he called to the palace of the Overseer. Outside of the door, Dolores, the Mayors new secretary, listened to the Mayors message. She then snuck off and reported to Somora, what she had learned.

Salsakor, was beyond irritated by the constant knocking, that had interrupted her quiet time. When she opened the door, her exasperated sigh was heard clearly, as she looked at the very fat visitor. "What do you want Barsantorack?" she asked, not even bothering to hide her anger at his presence. He glared at her.

"I am here to see Tremarack, not you," he told her, and tried to push his way into the house. He had no idea that she was as strong as she was, until he found himself again standing on the porch.

"You do not ever, for one second, think you can force your way into my house!" she yelled at him, her eyes flaming with her anger. He lost his temper.

"Get Tremarack, your husband, here, Now!" he roared at her, and she slammed the door in his face. He stood staring at the closed door, and his anger built. He was about to pound on it when it opened, and Tremarack looked at Barsantorack, and he was a very angry Bendine.

"Who the hell do you think you are to speak to my wife in that manner, you stupid ass!" Tremarack roared, and took a step towards Barsantorack, his fists clenched. Barsantorack took a step back, fear showing in his eyes. He held his hands up in front of him.

"Tremarack, calm yourself," Barsantorack told him. "I have come to speak with you about a very important matter. I do not think your wife need be part of it. I meant no disrespect, but it is vital that I speak with you." Tremarack looked at him, and his rage settled, slightly.

"What's so important that you cannot respect a Bendine home?" he demanded, his voice still holding some anger. Barsantorack bowed slightly.

"I am sorry about my behavior, but once you have heard what I have to say, you will see the importance," he told Tremarack, and moved closer, a sly smile on his lips. Tremarack watched him, and Barsantorack saw him thinking. "Tremarack," Barsantorack whispered, moving closer still; "this concerns the welfare of all of Bendine, and Ventoria!" Barsantorack glanced at Salsakor, who stood about eight feet behind her husband, her arms across her chest, and a glaring at Barsantorack.

"What could be so important?" Tremarack asked, and there was far less anger in his voice.

"Do not trust that liar!" Salsakor said loudly. "He only wants to use you in some way!" Barsantorack started to glare at her, but quickly changed his mind. He looked to Tremarack.

"I think it best we discuss this without her presence Tremarack," Barsantorack said softly; "and definitely, not on the front porch!" he added. Tremarack stared at him for a few moments, and then nodded.

"We can talk in my office," he told him, and turned around, reentering the house. Barsantorack smiled as he followed. Salsakor threw up her hands and stormed away.

"I'll not serve that fat liar, and I will not be here as long as he is in this house!" she told her husband. Very quickly, they both heard the slamming of the back door.

"There seems to be some question of who is the master of this house," Barsantorack said softly, and Tremarack glared at him as he opened the door to his office.

"Pay mind to your words Barsantorack. There is no question about that, ever!" he growled as the fat Bendine passed into the room.

"As you say Tremarack, but that is a prime example of why I am here. Do you have any brew?" His words all came as one question. He barely fit into chair in front of the desk. The chair groaned as Tremarack got a jug of brew from a cabinet behind the desk, and two mugs. Barsantorack immediately reached for the jug, and quickly poured his, and then Tremarack's mug full. He picked up his mug, and held it up to Tremarack. "To the betterment of all Bendine!" he toasted, and Tremarack hesitantly clicked mugs, and drank. His eyes staying on the more than simply obese Barsantorack. When they both had drank, Barsantorack much more than Tremarack, Barsantorack refilled his mug, and sat back. The chair groaned again.

"What is so important Barsantorack?" Tremarack asked as he sat. Barsantorack smiled slightly as he took another drink.

"We will start with your wife's behavior." He quickly held up his hand to stop Tremarack's objections. "Because of our Governor, the females of Bendine have forgotten their roles in the life of Bendine. They have forgotten their place. Why, under Borack's leadership, Salsakor would have been publicly whipped for behavior she displayed just now!" Tremarack looked to him, and Barsantorack leaned forward. "You know I speak the truth, but our leaders have taken it upon themselves to deprive the males of Bendine, the proper respect of our females!" Tremarack did not openly agree, but Barsantorack saw the wheels of thought turning in his head. "Do you know how this came to be?" Barsantorack pressed. "Because your grandfather, Dorack, did not stand up for his blood right of rule!" Tremarack began to object, but Barsantorack cut him off. "He allowed that half blood, Semirack, to be named Ruler without objection, and allowed the Governorship to take control of Bendine, that's how!" Tremarack stared at him for several moments, and then slowly nodded. Barsantorack smiled to himself. "It is time that the true blood line of Bendine retake that rule, and lead all Bendines to the proper life we had enjoyed for so long!" Barsantorack's voice got louder with each word. Tremarack nodded quicker this time. Barsantorack leaned closer, draining the mug he held, and refilled it. He quickly drained it again, and refilled it again. "You Tremarack, are the true blood line Ruler of Bendine, and it is time you took your proper place, as Ruler, and lead Bendine as it should be!"

Tremarack's eyes opened wide and he quickly drained his mug. He was lost in thought as he tried to refill his mug, but there was nothing left in the jug. "You do have more brew, don't you?" Barsantorack asked with a knowing smile, just before taking a drink from his mug.

———

The two Captains were sitting on a bench, in a small trash strewn, park like area, on the west side of Bandarson City. "I's sure dat a dwarf is foll'n us Porkligor," Rentaring whispered. "Brandaro mus be on to us!"

"Bah," the fat pirate told him. "Ya jus scared," Porkligor said, trying to pick what teeth he still had, for the residual meal bits he didn't want to lose. The skinny pirate looked to him, his face turning red with the anger he was feeling.

"I's ain't scared," he told Porkligor, trying to growl. "I's be'n careful, and I's knows a dwarfs foll'n us!" Rentaring looked around again. "Ya knows wha is said. Dat Pinsikar got dem spies everywhere." The fat Captain looked at him, and sneered.

"Ya scared," he told the skinny one. "Brandaro ain't got no reason to worry wid us. Didn't I just give him wha's he wan, even dow he's cheat's me?" he did growl with his question. Rentaring didn't hide his grin.

"Ya din plan dat well." he told Porkligor as he chuckled. Porkligor swung a back hand at him, which he easily dodged, and chuckled louder. "Wha made ya tink nine tiny girls nuff?" Rentaring chuckled louder, now out of reach of the fat one. Porkligor glared at him.

"Dar wasn't dat many good'uns to chose from," he growled. "Now we gotta plan to get even!" The listening dwarf, Pestikar, moved closer. He didn't think that either of the Captains could catch him, so he was very surprised when Porkligor suddenly reached out, with a speed Pestikar didn't think he possessed, and grabbed the dwarf around the neck with one hand. He lifted the dwarf up at eye level. "Well now, it seem dat you's was right afta all Rentaring." Porkligor growled. "Maybe dis little ting can tell us wha's we's needs to know." Pestikar's very frightened eyes looked into the deadly eyes of Porkligor, and he knew he was going to die.

The imp, Pratilatt, great grandson of Dalalatt, who had come to the Realm to help in the defense against Palakrine's forces, landed close to his mate, Wenlilatt. He could easily see that she was glaring at their son, Pegalatt. Glorilatt, his daughter, was standing farther back, and was grinning at her older brother with a little sister's knowing grin.

"What now?" Pratilatt asked, walking closer to Wenlilatt.

"He has decided that adding different colorings to waters of all the fountains at the palace, would make them much prettier!" his mate told him through clenched teeth. Pratilatt fought his grin, as he glanced at his daughter, who was nodding a grinning tattlers nod. Pratilatt was about to speak when Zackilatt, great grandson of Caratt and Selalatt, and was now the leader of the imps in the Realm, landed beside him. He was grinning.

"I guessed that your son is the artist of the fountains?" he stated, and asked, of Pratilatt. Pratilatt looked to him, and lost his battle with his own grin.

"So it would seem," he told Zackilatt with a attempt at controlling his chuckle.

"It was just a coloring spell," Pegalatt whined. "It will not affect the water in any way," he added. The three adult imps looked to him.

"You had better hope that the Overseer sees it that way Pegalatt," Zackilatt stated. "You know he is very fond of those fountains. They were Glornina's present to him when they wed!" Pegalatt dropped his head again.

"I ttttoooolllldddd you," Glorilatt said to her brother, teasingly. Wenlilatt looked at the girl.

"I will deal with you in a moment," she told her daughter, who looked surprised at her mother's tone of voice.

"What did I do?" she asked, her voice rising in octaves. Wenlilatt glared at her.

"What have I told you about being a tattle tale," Wenlilatt told her. Glorilatt pouted and sat down in a chair near her. Smoothing out the short skirt that somewhere along the line, had become the imps universal clothing. They still wore no clothing above the waist, but they all now wore some kind of a very short, double split skirt, below. Though, what the males wore was more a loin cloth than skirt, and was short enough that the cloth really didn't cover all that much. Zackilatt turned to Pratilatt.

"I have come with another purpose," he told his friend. Pratilatt lifted one brow. "The Overseer has sent word that the imps are to meet with him, when he soon returns from Neponia."

"What is this about?" Pratilatt asked as the two walked a short distance from the others'. Zackilatt shrugged slightly.

"I do not know for sure, but he has asked that the fairy folk, and imps, to meet with him." The leader told him. "I understand he met with the dragons, who have high magical powers, early this morning." Pratilatt lifted his other brow to join the first. He then looked to his son, who he knew to be young, and obviously still somewhat immature, but had more magical power than any other imp in the Realm.

"I will bring Pegalatt, for two reasons," he told Zackilatt. The Imp leader nodded, with a grin.

"I will let you know when the Overseer returns," Zackilatt told him, as he lived in the palace. Pratilatt and his family, lived with Drandysee, the Elder of the Guardians, working as aides, and messengers. Pratilatt nodded, and Zackilatt flew off.

"Why does Brandaro give you this chance?" Kris's hushed voice caused Isabella to jump. "What are you that he gives you, what he has never given to any female slave?" The girls voice held wariness, and fear. Isabella looked up into the eyes of the girl, and tried to smile.

"I have magical power, and he demands information I cannot allow him to have," she whispered. Kris looked into her eyes for several moments. She finally looked to the tight necklace around Isabella's neck, and then to the bracelets on her wrists.

"That explains the shielding jewelry," Kris said softly. Hope came to Isabella's eyes.

"Can you get them off of me?' she asked. Kris immediately began to shake her head.

"Only Brandaro, or Besaline, can do that," Kris told her. Again Isabella felt the harsh disappointment of her inability to get what she needed. "But, thankfully, they are not tracers, so I can get you out of here, and away from the very unpleasant tomorrow you face." Hope returned to Isabella's eyes as she looked to the smile of Kris. The girl beckoned her with her index finger. Isabella grinned as she rose from the wooden bed, and followed Kris to the corner she had first heard the girls voice. Kris pressed several different stones of the wall, and a large stone at floor level, swung inward, and an dark opening appeared. Kris indicated that Isabella should be quiet, and crawling on hands and knees, disappeared into the opening. Isabella glanced at the door of the cell, and then quickly followed the girl. The stone closed behind her, and she was in pitch blackness. "Don't worry," Kris told her, whispering into her ear. "You must be very quiet for a while. We will only be a wall away from most of the staff of the castle, and they would love to gain favor by giving Brandaro, both of us!"

"I understand," Isabella whispered back.

"Here," Kris said as a piece of cloth was forced into Isabella's hands. "Place the end in your mouth, and follow wherever it leads you, and stay on your hands and knees."

"Got it," Isabella replied and placed the cloth in her mouth. She almost gagged at the taste and smell of the cloth, but dutifully followed when she felt its pull.

. "Many, centuries ago, the Mearlies and the Elves, shared Elandif.," Telalon started the telling, trying to answer the question, by Namson, of what he and Wenzorn had talked of, at the beginning of this meeting.

"But, there came a building turmoil, caused by the greed of the current rulers of each race, to be the ultimate leader of both races," Wenzorn continued. "A war was fought between them, for that leadership. Those left of the Mearlies ended up fleeing to Neponia, where they were welcomed."

"Over time, the connection of the races was forgotten, except for a few, of each race," Telalon added. "Those few, of each, have kept the history of our cousins, quietly, and diligently."

"Why have you not told of this before?" Neponities asked, quietly. Wenzorn and Telalon shared a glance, and then Wenzorn turned to her.

"There is history of terrible things done, in all worlds," he told the Queen. Namson and Glornina nodded, with a glance to each other. "We have kept ours, for the day that we would again face our cousins, in peace and understanding."

"Then there is a common ancestry between you?" Namson asked. Both Telalon and Wenzorn nodded.

"We do not know for sure, how it came to be that there is a physical difference between us, but yes, it is known that we shared a common beginning," Telalon said. Wenzorn nodded his agreement.

———

When Namson and Glornina returned to the palace, after their meeting on Neponia, they were rather surprised at what Zachia told them. Telalon and his aides had stayed on Neponia, to reconnect with their lost cousins, the Mearlies, and to act as a intermediary between Neponia and the Realm

"Gordon has asked that he and several others, be spelled here, saying it was very important that you hear what one of the town of Zentler has to say!" Zachia told him. Namson glanced to Glornina, who shrugged.

"Alright, pass the word to the fairy folk and imps, that I am back, and our meeting should start soon." Zachia nodded. "How many am I to spell from Zentler?" he asked. Zachia didn't hide his grin too well.

"Gordon, Xanaporia, a young woman named Penelopy and two young men. A Marcus and Melsikan." Zachia told him. "Gordon seems quite upset about something," he added. "They're in his office." Namson nodded, and abruptly, five people stood in the middle of Namson's office.

"Namson, I'm sorry, but I think you really need to talk with this young man." Gordon said, putting his hand on Melsikan's shoulder. Namson nodded, grinning at the wide eyes of Penelopy and Marcus, as they stood, holding their stomachs, and looking around nervously.

"Why don't you all find a seat," Namson said softly. Xanaporia led Penelopy and Marcus to the sofa, as Gordon led Melsikan to the two chairs in front of the desk. Glornina sat with Xanaporia, but was watching the young man who sat next to Gordon. Xanaporia started to whisper into her ear, and Glornina's eyes began to widen as she looked to the two on the couch, and then to Melsikan.

"Alright Gordon, what's so important about this young man?" Namson asked, but Gordon didn't have a chance to answer.

"Are you familiar with the efforts of your predecessor, to find the history of Maltakrine?" Melsikan asked quietly. Namson looked to the him for a moment, and then nodded slowly. Melsikan smiled. "Do you know of the one called, Halispar?" Namson thought of all Mike had taught him concerning the history he had uncovered, and he finally came to the part that explained the individual Melsikan named.

"Yes, he was driven from the town of Pennes, after the disappearance of a couple of girls, wasn't he?" Namson said. Melsikan nodded.

"They were sisters," Melsikan said. "Neither left with the family, because they had run away from Halispar, his wife, and children. It would seem that one of the things Halispar and family had wanted, was to include eating them, after the other things they did." There were several gasps from the couch, and Namson lifted one brow. Melsikan nodded. "They, the two sisters, had both been impregnated by Halispar before they managed to get away from him. They managed their escape by going deeper into the ruins, where none of the family would dare venture, simply because they were cowards." Melsikan stopped for a breath and Namson sat forward, thinking he was getting an idea where Melsikan's story was leading. "While they explored the inner regions of the ruins, they stumbled into a second portal, that took them directly into the castle of the Keeper of Magic,

Belgarn." Namson realized that this story was not to go as he thought it would. "They managed to get all the way through the portal, I guess it had just enough power left to it that they could make the passage. Anyway, they stayed in the background of the palace, actually assuming jobs in the kitchen, and apparently, were never questioned about their presence, until after they had both delivered the child they had been forced to bear." Melsikan had not yet moved his eyes from Namson's.

"The child of Tepria, the younger of the two sisters, was a girl, and gained the favor of Stellagarn, the youngest of Belgarn's daughters. The older sisters child, a boy, did not fare as well, and ended up being employed in the stables. What neither sister had known before, was that Dremlitan, the older one, had a latent magical ability, and with the forced mating with Halispar, the child, Demastan, developed a slightly less than a medium level, magical talent. Dremlitan made sure that the boy never showed his powers, to anyone. He grew up, and found love with one of the scullery maids. They had but one child, a girl, Dremlastar. She grew, and married one of Prannope's sorcerers, and they had but one child, Dramsatar." Here Melsikan looked around the room, to each set of eyes, finally returning to Namson's. "Each single child creating but one child, and with each new child, the magical talent grew stronger, and each held fast to the idea that they had to keep their talents from the eyes of others." Namson nodded as a grin played with the corners of his mouth. "I think you see where I am going." Melsikan smiled as he looked to Namson." I was born but seventeen years ago, to Dramatar and a sorceress, Melsitaren, who, as a mere child, had escaped after Pennope was banished," he told them all. Out of the corner of his eye, Namson saw his wife start to call to the South East Domain. Melsikan's smile grew as he kept looking to Namson, never looking to Glornina. "She will find that what I say concerning my parents is true," he told Namson quietly. Namson looked to Glornina. She looked back to him, and nodded.

"How strong in magic are you?" Namson asked. Melsikan's smile shrank to nothing.

"Not strong enough to stop the bastards from taking Isabella," he hissed.

"According to what I heard, the bandits surprised Melsikan from behind, and beat him severely, before Isabella was dragged from her house." Gordon said as he placed his hand on the boys shoulder. "They are in love and from what Isabella had told me several days before the attack, Melsikan had asked her to marry him and she had enthusiastically said yes," he added. Namson nodded as he looked to Melsikan.

"I am sorry for you, but know that we are doing everything we can to get her back," Namson told him, and Melsikan nodded.

"I know, I've been listening," he told Namson. The Overseer nodded and looked to the two on the couch.

"What is your two's connection to all of this?" he asked them.

"I am Isabella's cousin, and she told me of her powers." Penelopy said quietly. Namson nodded and looked to Marcus.

"I'm married to her," he said simply, pointing to Penelopy. "I never knew, or even thought of the possibility that there were people with magical abilities living in Zentler, though there had been moments, when things have happened that I couldn't explain. Penelopy told me a lot, on our wedding night, and I've been getting surprised every moment or two, since," he added and Namson chuckled. He returned his eyes to Melsikan.

"Can you talk to her?" he asked softly. Melsikan shook his head.

"I had chosen not to, even though I knew she was a strong magical power. At least not until we were wed. I have tried since awakening from being knocked unconscious, but she has not answered" Melsikan's voice was very quiet. "I had been beaten unconsciousness before I could, when she was taken." Melsikan said with a quiet rage. Namson again nodded his understanding.

"Alright, I've got a meeting with the fairy folk and imps soon, so I'm going to send you back to Zentler, but if you sense anything, or she does manage to contact you, make sure I know immediately!" Melsikan nodded. Glornina, who had come from the couch, placed her hand on his shoulder.

"You can call to me anytime. If we learn anything, I will tell you as soon as I can," she told him. Melsikan smiled.

"Thank you," he told her. The five gathered together in the center of the room. Namson nodded to them, and they disappeared. Namson rose from his chair and Glornina came into his arms.

"The hell that young man must be feeling," she said into his shoulder. He nodded and gave her a small squeeze.

"Not as much I fear, as she does," he said, and they went to the meeting with the imps and fairy folk.

Chapter Four

Calteen, leader of the fairy folk of the Realm, and his mate, Salear, sat on a limb, watching the young fairies, pixies, and faxlies, playing fairy tag. It was a very fast, and sometimes dangerous game, that all fairy folk loved to play. The rules were simple. There were twelve to fifteen players, and at least three who were *It*, at the same time. Those who were *It*, could not tag each other, or any, the other *It's*, were chasing. They were all flying very fast, and there was always the chance of collision with each other, or a tree.

"Have you decided who is to go to Neponia yet?" Salear asked, watching a young pixie who was in pursuit of a faxlie, to tag him. Anymore, with the pairings between fairies and pixies, and throwing in the faxlies, most of the fairy folk of the Valley, Plain, and Realm, were now faxlies. The only way to tell the difference was the wings. Two wings, a pixie, four wings, a fairy, and six wings, a faxlie.

"There have been many to volunteer," Calteen said as he and Salear ducked out of the way of the two speeding game players, who almost knocked them from their perch. "Most of them very young," he added as they sat back up, their eyes still following the two players.

"The young will need guidance," Salear said quietly. Calteen nodded, and then laughed as the pixie did an amazing flip over, at a very high speed, surprising the faxlie with a profound tagging. A cheer rose from the spectators as the pixie sped from the wide eyed faxlie. The other dozen or so percipients of the game congratulating the pixie. The faxlie put a smiling scowl on his face and eyed a very pretty fairy. He gave chase as she squealed and fled from him.

"That is why I'm sending Porlear, Belear, Calear and Pirteen." Salear nodded as she laughed at the antics of two new players. "I had hoped that Miteen would have volunteered, but he didn't." Salear looked to her mate in surprise.

"I just talked with Glolear earlier this morning and she said that he had," she told Calteen. It was his turn to look at her in surprise.

"He hasn't told me that," he told her. Salear shrugged and then looked around.

"He's over there," she said, pointing across the playing field. "Maybe you should check with him?" she suggested. He grinned at her, lifted from the limb, and started across the playing field. She followed. "I'm coming too. Remember what happened the last time you and our son talked." Her voice held a certain amount of worry, reproachfulness, and humor.

"That was something completely different," he shouted to her as they dived out of players ways. She laughed at what they were doing, and his words.

Glolear poked her mate in the ribs and pointed to Calteen and Salear coming towards them, threading their way between the players. "Looks like your mother told him," she said into his ear. He grinned and nodded, watching his parents as they unwittingly became part of the game of fairy tag. They laughed with all the others', as the faxlie tagged Salear instead of the fairy he had been chasing, and she promptly tagged Calteen, and beat a hasty retreat. He roared his surprise, and chased after the fairy that was being chased before. "Does he really think he can catch her?" Glolear asked. Miteen laughed out loud.

"Do not ever sell my father short. He may be old, but he's sneaky," he told her, and then gave a cheer of support to Calteen. Salear popped up behind the couple.

"How's he doing?" she asked as she settled next to Miteen.

"You know him," he told her. "He won't quit until he tags somebody!" Miteen laughed with Glolear and his mother. Calteen laughed as he suddenly flipped over and shot off in a strange direction. The female fairy didn't know what to do and turned right into the waiting hand of the leader of the fairy folks of the Realm. "Told you he was sneaky!"

Miteen cheered with the other spectators. The fairy gave Calteen a hug, and set off to find a victim of her own. Calteen flew to them and received a hero's kiss from his mate, and a hug from Glolear. Miteen held out his arm and Calteen shared an arm clasp with his son. "I swear, the older you get, the trickier you get," he told his father. "Why didn't you ask me to go to Neponia?" Calteen looked to Miteen and tried to patiently answer.

"I put out a call for volunteers," he told him. Miteen nodded as he dropped his father's arm.

"I heard that, but why didn't you ask me personally?" he asked. Glolear and Salear shared worried glances, because this was the same as the start of the last conversation the two had had, and that had ended in a shouting match.

"Well," Calteen started, badly hiding his sarcasm. "When the Overseer called the meeting for the imps and fairy folk yesterday, I tried to find you because I wanted you with me, but you seemed to have something else of more importance to do, so I assumed you weren't interested in going!" Miteen began to cloud up with his own irritation and Salear and Glolear pushed their way between them.

"Miteen," Glolear stated. "I love you with my entire being, but there are times you can be so stubbornly arrogant, you try even my patience!" He looked to her with surprise. "Don't give me those big eyes. We have talked about this, and you promised to try harder, after the last conversation you had with your father, and you were wrong then too!" she told him, her hands still on his chest.

"I'm sorry my son," Salear added; "but Glolear is right, but it was not just you who was wrong." She looked into Calteen's widening eyes. "You are supposed to be the leader of the fairy folk, but you can't even talk with your son without sarcasm, or ridicule," she told him, anger flashing into her eyes for just a moment. She turned to look at Miteen. "Do you want to go to Neponia?" she asked. Miteen nodded, glancing at his father. "Are you willing to listen to, *and obey*, your fathers ideas about what is to be done by the fairy folk sent there?" Again Miteen nodded.

"Without the attitude?" Glolear asked quickly, with feeling. Miteen glared at her for about a split second, and then nodded. Salear turned back to her mate.

"Are you willing to try and not be sarcastic anymore?" she asked quietly. He looked at her for a moment and then glanced at his son. He placed his hands on Salear's waist and nodded as he looked to Miteen.

"I'm sorry Miteen, I should not have treated you like that. I would like it if you were to go to Neponia." Calteen said. Miteen nodded and a small smile came to him.

"I want to go, and I'm sorry too," he told his father, and the rest.

"Way to go mama!" Meglear said as she and her mate, Morteen, landed on the limb. She grinned at her older brother. "Now you know why there are Queens who lead the Plains and Valley fairy folks!" The other four groaned at her words.

"There is to be a meeting this afternoon, with all who wish to go to Neponia," Calteen said, trying to ignore his daughters obsession with establishing a Queen to rule the Realm fairy folk. He knew that she wanted to be that Queen and that thought frightened not only him, but a great many of the fairy folk as well! "I would like you to come with me. I want you to be this missions leader." Miteen's eyes opened slightly as he nodded yes.

They all ignored Meglear's groan.

───ᦔᦔᦔ᭟᭟᭟───

Zachia sent a messenger to Zaclitile, asking that he and the other young dragons, with the greater magical powers, to meet with him in the rear yard of the palace. He also sent messengers to the younger imps, fairy folk, trolls, ogres, eagles, bats, and elves. All those who had the higher magical talents. He also had Emma, who was a powerful talker, to call and ask Melsikan if he could teleport. Melsikan told her he had never tried, but was willing to try, He was quite happy when he appeared next to Zachia. Zachia told him to return to Zentler and try to bring Marcus and Penelopy with him. Seconds later, the three stood together on the rear terrace. Melsikan went to Zachia, unaffected by the trip, but there was a rather sick look on both Marcus and Penelope's face.

"Are they going to be doing this to us a lot?" Marcus's groaning whisper asked his new wife, as his hands tried to comfort his sickened stomach. Zachia smiled at them.

"Maybe we'll get used to it?" she whispered back and then swallowed, hard.

"Yes, you will," Emma said with a grin, as she handed them each a small glass of juice. "Here, drink this, it will help your stomachs." The two almost smiled, and then quickly drank the juice. Within seconds they were smiling, their stomachs no longer trying to come up out of them. Suddenly, Glorian and Braxton, from the Canyon, and Michele and Crendoran, from Calisonnos, appeared near them, and they both jump at the sudden appearance. The four new comers laughed as they joined Zachia, Emma, and Melsikan. Many others began to appear and each surprised the two, who were unaccustomed to people just popping out of nowhere. Talk quickly had begun as the races began to gather. Some by wing, some by foot. Marcus and Penelopy stood with their mouths hanging open as they looked from one of the races to the next. Emma and Glorian came to them.

"Come on, you two are part of this now, you might as well partake of the discussions," Emma told them. Glorian nodded her agreement.

"Is that a real unicorn?" Penelopy whispered her question to Emma.

"Is that a Dragon?" Marcus asked, and his voice came nowhere near a whisper. Everyone, human and other, laughed, and Marcus and Penelopy both blushed.

"Yes, to both questions," Zachia told them. "You will get a chance to meet them all, after this meeting is over," he told them. They nodded and took the seats they had been shown. Their heads down slightly, with their embarrassment.

Isabella had no idea how far she had crawled, but her knees hurt, and she was quite sure they were badly scrapped. She also knew that the taste of the cloth in her mouth was becoming unbearable. The cloth slackened, and she stopped. There came a soft grinding noise behind her, followed by a soft clunk. Suddenly, a match flared and Isabella had to squint against even that little bit of a light. She spit the offending cloth from her mouth and tried to look around. She saw that Kris had already lit one lamp and was starting to light a second. She looked behind her and all she could see was another stone wall. She slowly got to her feet, continuing to look around. In front of her, centered in the large cavern she was in, was a fire pit. Kris had gotten all of the lamps lit and was now starting a fire. Isabella looked up and saw a small darkening patch of the sky, far above her.

"Where are we?" she asked, trying to ignore the residual taste of the cloth. Kris looked at her with a huge grin.

"My home, or as much of one as I really remember ever having," she told her as the fire began to grow. "Come closer to the fire, and I'll see if I can find you some clothes to wear." Isabella welcomed the heat of the fire, for the thin dress she wore did little to keep her warm.

"You live here?" Isabella asked as she looked closer to the large room, her hands rubbing together, over the growing fire. She could now see two beds, spaced a distance from each other, not too far from her, behind and to her left. There was a table and several chairs, with a candle on the table, to her right. She could hear a running stream not too far away.

"Yep," Kris answered as she came around an outcropping, some clothes wadded in her arms. "These may not be as good as what you're used to, but they're all I got that might fit you," she said as she held out the bundle. "You're bigger than I am, in certain places," she added with a grin. Isabella took the clothes and looked around for someplace to change. Kris started to chuckle.

"You've been stripped naked in front of a whole room, mostly men, and you're worried about me?" she asked. Isabella realized her truth, and laughed as she pulled the simple dress up over her head. She dug through the clothes Kris had given her and quickly realized there were no under garments. She started to pull on the breeches when she saw that Kris was staring at her body. There was a strange hinted glint to the girls eyes, and Isabella was surprised that she felt no dislike of it. She felt no embarrassment from her stare. She pulled the shirt down over her head, feeling better that she was again covered. A sweater, of some type of material she didn't know, came next, and a vest on top of that. The shirt was tight across her breasts, and the breeches tight on her hips, but the long, lose sweater and vest, concealed both situations well.

"Well, you ought to be hungry by now," Kris said as she looked to the pots near the fire. "Let's see what I can throw together." Kris took one of the pots and went to the stream that Isabella had heard, but had not seen earlier. She dipped the pot and brought it back to the fire, hanging it from the chain that hung from the tripod, over the fire. "I'm not making any guarantees here, but I should have enough for us both," she said, and went to a large box looking chest that was sunk partway in the stream. "Keeps things colder this way," she said as she lifted the lid and pulled a few things from the interior. "There should be some glasses in that cabinet there," Kris told her, pointing to cabinet, hung on the wall behind the table. "There should be some wine in there as well," she added. Isabella started towards the table and her bare feet felt the cold of the stone floor.

"Ah, Kris," she started to ask, and Kris looked up to her; "do you have anything I can put on my feet?" she asked. Kris looked at her and then down to her feet.

"Damn, I forgot," she said. "Yeah, I've got something. They kinda wrap around your foot and then tie to hold them in place," she told Isabella. She disappeared around the outcropping and returned quickly. "Sorry, it's the best I could do in a hurry," she told Isabella, who smiled at the girl.

"Believe me, they're fine," she told Kris. She sat down in one of the chairs and put the foot wear on. Kris went back to the fire and pulling a knife from the end of a cut off log, began to cut up what she had pulled from the box. Isabella found the glasses and the wine, of which there was several bottles, as well as bottles of other liquors. She also saw the box that sat on the floor, near the cabinet. It was filled with pouches, as well as wooden, and metal boxes. Isabella realized that they probably contained money, or gold, or jewels, most likely stole from the peoples of this city. She turned back towards the table as saw that Kris was watching her. Neither said anything for a few moments. Finally, Isabella smiled, and shrugged. She went to the table, wiped the dust from the glasses, and poured the wine into them. She carried the two glasses to where Kris was cutting up the last of what was going into the pot.

"Probably best you don't ask what's in there," she told Isabella, who nodded her agreement. Kris stuck the knife back into the log end, and took one of the glasses. "Here's to Brandaro's rage when he finds you gone in the morning!" Kris announced, and held up her glass. Isabella looked at her and felt her fear return. Kris smiled. "Don't worry, there's only two people in all of Bandarson, that know of this place, and the other ones dead," she told Isabella calmly. "Now drink up, you're safe from that big bastard." Isabella tried to smile, and touched her glass to Kris's, and drank. Right after her drink, she looked at Kris closely for the first time. The girl had blondish hair, cut very short, like a boys would be, and was almost a head shorter than Isabella. She had blue eyes, that truly sparkled when she smiled. Isabella felt a sadness for the thought that the girl probably had not had much to be smiling about in her life. "Come on, let's sit down. This stew going to take some time to get done," Kris told her and they headed for the table. After they had sat, Kris reached for the wine bottle and refilled her glass.

"How old are you Kris?" Isabella asked. The girl took a drink and looked at her. She finally shrugged.

"I don't know for sure," she told Isabella. "Fifteen, sixteen, somewhere in there I think." Kris took another drink and her eyes turned angry. "Pelteran would know for sure, but Brandaro and Telposar tore him to pieces a few years ago, when they caught him trying to steal some food from the kitchen. The bastards laughed at his screams," she hissed and quickly took a drink and wiped her eyes. Isabella held her glass in both hands that rested on the table and leaned closer to the girl.

"Who was Pelteran?" she asked softly, watching Kris carefully. Kris didn't answer right away and Isabella was about to repeat the question.

"He was my older brother," she said quietly. "He's the one to find this place, and all the passageways throughout the castle." Kris took another long drink. "Our parents, school teachers, had been captured, and killed, because Brandaro didn't want his people to be able to read or write. My mother had been forced to spend the time until her death, as a bed whore for the guards. I was very young when Pelteran snuck me here and took care of me. He taught me to read and write. To talk without sounding like a babbling idiot, which most do in this domain. He even explained what was happening when I changed from a young girl to a mature one." Tears were being fought, and the tears were winning. Kris suddenly put her face in her hands and silently wept. Isabella came around the table to put her arms around the girl. But, as soon as Isabella's hands touched the girl, she received some kind of a jolt! At the same moment, in the Realm, as Zachia was talking to those gathered, Penelopy screamed out; "Isabella?" Complete silence followed her outburst, as all looked to her very wide, and tear filling eyes. The sun had begun to set in the west.

The Mearlies had managed to set up three beds for Telalon and his two aides, in the building in which they had been reunited. They had arraigned some free standing curtains to isolate them from the rest of the room, for privacy. They also supplied food, and cooks. There had been some difficulty trying to figure out a way for Telalon to get to see the different stages of the Power Stones assemblage, because there was no way the over six foot tall elf was going to fit into the tunnels, that were very wide, but only four foot tall, and at his age, he couldn't crawl through them. They finally came up with a simple wagon. Telalon could sit, leaning back slightly, in the wagon, and be pulled through the tunnels to the different areas.

Neponities and Cartope visited them every day, questioning Telalon about elves, the Realm, and the powers of those who dwelt in the other five more powerful domains. Telalon did not hold much back from them, but couldn't stop himself from worrying about all the information they sought.

Namson had supplied two orbs, one for Neponities, and the other for Telalon. Telalon was then able to stay in contact with Perolon, on Elandif, Phemlon, in the

Realm, and of course, the Overseer. The main thing that Namson had wanted to know, was if a smaller version of the Power Stones could be made, and how long that would take. Wenzorn's answer stayed consistent; *It takes two years to make a Power Stone, no matter its size.* To say this frustrated Namson would be a very serious understatement! He then had Telalon try to find out exactly, the multiplying factor of the Power Stones. He turned to the elves of the Realm, to figure out how big, meaning height, width, and depth, a Milky Quartz amulet had to be, to counter the bandits spells. This was not an easy undertaking, for they had no idea of the level of magical power, of the average bandit.

The panel of talkers had started to center on reconnecting with Daridar, but her anger, and plans of revenge on Pestikar, kept her attention, and she couldn't be distracted from it.

Then Namson received word of Penelope's outcry.

———〜✻❈✿❈✻〜———

Brandaro woke with a powerful hunger. Morselia and Caratelia were hard pressed to stay up with him. When they all were completely satisfied, they rose and went to the bathing pools, where naked female slaves bathed them. The gropings the slaves received, were expected and enjoyed, and were not just from Brandaro. The same slaves, flushed from the warmth of the water, and the pleasure they had been given, dried them and helped them into robes. The three left the bathing room and entered the dining room, where their very large breakfasts awaited them. They ate with a hunger that surprised all that served them. They finished their breakfast and returned to their quarters, where more slaves, both male and female, helped them dress. These slave received fondlings as well, and they too enjoyed what they were given. The three were in a very good mood when they arrived in the room with the large, resplendent couch. Once seated, Brandaro looked to the captain of the guard, with a deadly eye. "Bring the girl to me," he ordered. The Captain bowed, took two other guards, and left the room. Morselia and Caratelia giggled quietly for the anticipated enjoyment of what Brandaro was going to do to the girl. The guards returned quickly, without Isabella. They all wore a surprised, and very fearful look on their faces.

"Lord Brandaro," the captain announced, a tremor in his voice. "She was not in the cell." Brandaro stared at him for several seconds and no one liked the color of his face when he spoke.

"What do you mean, she was not in the cell?" he asked, in a growl. The Captain was looking for someplace to hide, though he knew there would be none for him. "How could she not be in the cell!" he roared standing, his fists clenched. The Captain and two soldiers trembled when the Captain replied.

"We went to the cell, unlocked the door and entered. It was empty!" The Captain tried to sound authoritive, but it came out more of a whine. Brandaro was trying to control himself and was not succeeding well.

"Show me!" he ordered, as started for the door. The three soldiers scurried ahead of him. Morselia and Caratelia followed, their faces showing the same anger as Brandaro's. When they all arrived at the cell, the door stood wide open. The guards stepped out of the way as Brandaro glared at the Captain. "You did not relock the door?" he asked, his voice close to a yell. "What if she had found a way to not be seen by you? You leave the door open and she simply walks away!" Brandaro entered the cell. He quickly looked around, including up. He then closed his eyes. His hands lifted slightly and he muttered a spell. Morselia and Caratelia smiled, knowing that he would soon locate the girl, because of the necklace and bracelets she wore. A growl issued from Brandaro's throat as he spun around, and charged out of the door. He turned and stormed off, towards the slave masters quarters, the women in hot pursuit, wearing confused looks. The Captain and two soldiers followed, very cautiously. As he neared the door he sought, his huge fist shot out and the door shattered inward. The few slaves in the room, screamed, and fell to the floor, covering themselves as best they could. Besaline looked into the enraged eyes of Brandaro and she felt great fear. "You did not put tracers on her?" he roared at her. Besaline slowly shook her head.

"My Lord, you did not order tracers Lord Brandaro," she whispered, backing until a wall stopped her. Brandaro was breathing very hard and Besaline could have sworn there was steam coming from his nostrils. She began to shake uncontrollably. Silence came to the room, except for Brandaro's labored breathing. Morselia and Caratelia looked back and forth between Besaline, with anger, to

Brandaro, with worry. Slowly, Brandaro regained control. He turned to the Captain.

"I want this castle, and the entire city, turned inside out," he stated with a calm that surprised all. "Every house, barn, shed, or anything else that could hide someone. Every nook and cranny, torn to pieces until that girl is found!" Brandaro looked to the frightened Captain. "Do you understand me?" he growled. The Captain nodded rapidly. Then he and the two soldiers beat a very fast retreat. "Get me Telposar, Now!" Brandaro roared to anyone, and left the room. Morselia and Caratelia followed, sharing very frightened, yet angry looks.

Isabella woke to the sound of a pans being moved around. She didn't immediately open her eyes, letting her ears try to figure out where she was. She smiled as the memories of the previous evening came to her. She then frowned and her eyes opened, looking around, as the memory of the jolt she had felt when she touched Kris, came to her. She sat up and saw Kris at the fire, getting things ready to start breakfast. The girl looked over her shoulder and smiled.

"About time you woke up," she said as she stood and went to the other side of the fire. She took a cup from one of the hooks that were on a single braced board, stood up on end, and grabbed the coffee pot and filled a cup. "I thought you were going to sleep all day," she added as she brought the cup to her. Isabella was shocked to see that the girl was not only naked and very obviously older than Isabella had first thought, but she didn't seem to be bothered by that fact in the slightest.

"Thank you," Isabella said as she took the offered cup. Kris smiled and turned back to the fire area. She felt a chill and looked down at herself. She then remembered that she too had shed her clothing before getting into bed and she was naked as well. She took a sip of the coffee, cringing with the realization that the girl did not make very good coffee, as she looked around for her clothes. She saw them laying across a small table, just feet from her. She threw back the covers and started to dress. She glanced to where Kris was getting dressed as well.

"What time is it?" she asked, and Kris laughed.

"Does that really matter?" she asked back. "What matters is that by now, Brandaro has found you not where he left you, and is probably so mad he will most likely destroy something!" Kris's laughter fueled Isabella's smile. It was then that Isabella noticed that Kris was putting on different clothes then yesterday. By the time the girl turned and walked back to her, she looked like a boy. "You need to stay here. Don't go exploring, okay?" Kris asked with a smile. "I'm going to get us something for breakfast. You don't mind meat and eggs do you, maybe a potato?" she asked as she turned and pulled a hat and coat from a hook. Isabella smiled as she shook her head.

"That sounds wonderful," she told the smiling girl. As soon as the hat and coat were on, Kris looked to her and her expression turned very serious.

"I mean it, stay here. Don't go wandering around, because Brandaro's going to have every soldier, and their brother and sister, out looking for you, and you don't know the tunnels. Stay put, okay?" Isabella nodded with a grin.

"I assure you, I'm not going anywhere. I'll see if I can make some better coffee while you're gone," she added softly. Kris grinned and nodded.

"Sorry, I never could get that to come out right," she said as she pointed to a container not far from the fire pit. "Grounds are in that container," she said, and then turned and started to walk away. "I shouldn't be too long," she said as she disappeared around a large rock. Isabella smiled, nodded to herself, and took her cup to the fire.

Daridar had been forced to wait several days before she could obtain her revenge. Pestikar had been away from the hovel most of the time, and when he did show up, he was very nervous, and after eating and drinking his brandy, quickly, he would go straight to bed and to sleep, not even looking at her. This only added to her anger. Then her time came. He arrived home and ate a quick meal. While doing this, his eyes repeatedly looked her over. She smiled at him, but he did not know what that smile truly meant. She dutifully cleaned the dishes and table, while he sipped some brandy that he had made some kind of deal for. Finally, the time came and he took her arm and led her to the bed. She removed her gown and lay down. He all but tore his clothes off and started to climb on top of her. She suddenly jerked her knees up until they were just under her chin, pressed together.

"What are you doing?" he asked, surprised.

"When you first bed me, you made the effort to give me pleasure," she told him gently. "But since, you have used me as a parsha. Well, if that is what I am to be, you will pay me as a parsha, or, make the effort to please me!" she yelled at him. His face turned red with his anger.

"You are mine," he told her, his rage clear in his voice. "I will have you as I want, and when I want," he yelled and penetrated her, laying on her shins. She shook her head.

"Not without paying or proving!" she screamed. With her hands on her thighs, she shoved him from her as hard as she could. This not only lifted him off, and out of her, it lifted him from the bed and over the end of it, into the wall not too far away. She was right after him, picking up the large piece of stove wood she had placed by the bed. "Not without pay or proof," she screamed again and hit him on the side of his head, hard! She didn't look at him again, or worry about him. She rose from the bed, dropping the piece of wood. She put her gown on and returned to the table. She sat in the chair that he had claimed was his, and picked up the glass of brandy he had been sipping. She started to sip from it. The more she sipped, the wider her smile became. Not used to the brandy, it did not take long and she passed out in the chair, and did not wake until late the next morning. She dealt with her need for the outhouse, and then began to make herself something to eat. She didn't worry about

Pestikar, assuming he had already left. It was well into the afternoon before she found him, laying in a pool of his own blood, at the foot of the bed. She looked at him for a moment, and then smiled slightly.

"I told you," she said, and then started to think of how she was going to get rid of the body. Of course, in Bandarson City, a dead dwarf found in the streets, was not an uncommon thing, so she wasn't too worried. She went back to the table and the brandy, only this time, she sipped slowly and actually enjoyed the taste, and effect. After it had been dark for some time, she dragged his body to an alley and left it there. She returned home and cleaned up the mess he had made with his blood. She then went to the loose floor board, under his side of the bed, he hadn't thought she knew of. She was very surprised at the amount of money, gold and jewels she found hidden there. She also found papers, a lot of them. She could only but barely read and the papers meant nothing to her, so, she put them into the stove. She didn't realize that those papers were proof against Porkligor and Rentaring, that Brandaro would have paid her handsomely for. Her smile grew and grew as she envisioned her future. If she was going to be treated as a parsha, she was going to be the best! She realized that she needed to organize not only the dwarf females, but all females who were treated as parsha's, and set prices for their labors. *Yes*, she thought to herself, *I am going to be the best parsha, ever!*

Coursel, leader of the trolls of the Plain, walked into the dining room of the castle on the Plain, surprising Quansloe and Hannah. "Keeper?" Coursel asked loudly. "Can you send me toooo the elves ooooof the Realm?" Quansloe and Hannah exchanged quick glances.

"Why would you want to go there?' Quansloe asked calmly, but carefully.

"Because I think I have foooound soooomething that will soooolve the questiooooon oooof the Milky Quartz sizing," the troll told him. Again, the Mistress and Keeper of the Plain, looked to each other.

"I have a turn coming on the talkers panel," Hannah said, with a small shrug, and Quansloe nodded.

"We will take you Coursel," Quansloe said, and the two finished their coffee and stood. "I am quite sure the Overseer will want to hear what you have to say as well." Coursel nodded and the three disappeared. They appeared in the main hall of the palace, and Hannah headed for the area where the talkers tables were. Quansloe and Coursel headed for Namson's office. They were not prepared for the activity in that office. Coursel and Quansloe stood to one side, as someone or another, was constantly going into, or out of the office. Finally they heard Namson.

"Could everyone just stop moving and be quiet for a moment please?" he called out and everyone froze. Carla was closest to him, so Quansloe leaned to her.

"What's happening?' he whispered and she looked to him with surprise.

"You haven't heard?' she asked. Quansloe looked at her with that, *are you serious*, look. "One of the girls who were kidnapped from Zentler, managed to make some kind of contact with Penelopy of Zentler, while she was here at the palace," she told him and slipped out the door.

"Alright Penelopy, try to tell me again, and hopefully I can hear you this time." Namson said. Quansloe looked to the girl with wide eyes, for he recognized the name. That's when he saw Gordon kneeling on one knee, beside the girl on one side, and Marcus kneeling on the other. Xanaporia was standing behind, with her hands on the girls shoulders.

"I was sitting, trying to understand what Zachia was telling everybody, when suddenly," the girls voice broke with her tears.

"It's alright Penelopy, take your time," Namson tried to calm her.

"I saw Isabella, just as clear as though she stood in front of me!" Penelopy raced her words out and then she was crying again, still looking at Namson. "She was right in front of me and she was looking very concerned about something, and was dressed in some very strange clothes." Penelopy managed through her tears. Namson gave her a few seconds.

"Could you see what concerned her?" he asked softly and Penelopy shook her head, as she wiped the tears from her face, then suddenly looked to the Overseer.

"She was in a cave, or something like one, and she was reaching her arms out, like she was going to give someone a hug," Penelopy said quite loudly. "But it was only a split second and then she was gone. She's alive!" Penelopy told them all, and then looked at Melsikan. "She alive," she told him again, softly. He smiled and nodded.

"That sounds like Isabella," Xanaporia said. "She was always trying to give comfort, or assistance, to somebody." Gordon looked to his wife, again surprised at how much she seemed to know about Isabella. Glornina, who had been standing next to Namson, leaned down and whispered in his ear. He nodded.

"Tell them to keep at it. We have to reestablish a link with this Daridar," he told her. She nodded and was obviously talking to someone on the panel. Namson looked to Gordon and then Marcus. "Take her home, but notify me immediately if she has another sensing," he told them. Xanaporia added her nod to theirs as she helped Penelopy from the chair. Melsikan moved closer to the four and they disappeared. Namson looked to Zachia. "That boy has more power than he showing and I don't think he's telling us all that he knows." Zachia allowed a half grin to join his nod. By this time, Quansloe and Coursel had managed to get near the desk.

"Overseer," Quansloe called softly. Namson looked up and smiled.

"Quansloe, Coursel, what brings you two?" he asked. Quansloe looked to Coursel.

"It's your idea," he told the troll and moved back so Coursel could get closer.

"I think I have foooound an answer toooo the Milky Quartz sizing, and I need toooo talk with the elves aboooout it," he told Namson. The Overseer looked a little surprised as he looked around the room. He pointed to the backs of two elves leaving the room.

"There goes Phemlon and Phelilon," he told the troll. "Let me know what is decided," he told them as Quansloe and Coursel chased after the two elves. They caught them just before they exited the building.

―――――――――

"Phemlon," Quansloe called to the elves, causing them to turn. "Coursel has a thought on the Milky Quartz. May we have a moment of your time?" he asked as he and the troll stopped before them. Phemlon looked to Coursel and smiled.

"Of course," he told them. He pointed to the reading room. "How about in here?" he asked and the troll nodded, and led the way into the room. Phelilon closed the door as the troll began to speak. When he had finished, there were two wide eyed elves, wearing very silly grins on their faces, and a smiling Keeper of the Plain. There was also a smiling Baldor as he snuck off from the window, and reported to Somora.

Pinsikar scurried from the castle, heading for his hovel. He was very scared now. He hadn't heard from Pestikar in days. Brandaro was going insane with his rage over the loss of the female, and Telposar and that Belidaria, were on a gleeful rampage of their own. This was not the time for a dwarf to be out and about in the city! He was being very careful as he eased his way from the castle and onto the road that led to his hovel. He had traveled some distance when he ran into Daridar, as she was coming the other way. She had been talking with her mother, who was quite willing to support her daughter in her quest to lead all females to a better treatment by the males. He tried to grab her shoulders as he shouted at her.

"Where is Pestikar?" he yelled, forgetting his fear to be quiet, and the fact that dwarf females were actually larger than the males, and stronger. He was very surprised when he saw the rage that suddenly appeared in her eyes. She shoved him from his unsecured grasp of her, and came towards him with her fists clenched.

"I am not subject to you anymore Pinsikar," she screamed at him, and swung her fist at him. He ducked the punch and backed farther from her, wide eyed. She continued towards him. "I know not where that scum is. He, and you, have treated me as a parsha, and I am no longer subject to him either," she continued to yell and threw another punch at him. Daridar's rage was enforced by the confusion in Pinsikar's eyes. She knew that females always obeyed their males, and she was feeling the power of her rebellion! Pinsikar turned and ran back towards the castle in his confusion, and fear. Daridar gave chase, screaming curses at him. As they reentered the city proper and neared the castle, the two guards at the gate saw the race, and laughed at the fleeing Pinsikar. The two gate guards let Pinsikar pass into the court yard and then blocked the still screaming Daridar with crossed lances in one hand, and their other hands on the hilts of their swords. She screamed her frustrations at the two guards. Their laughter only infuriated her more. Finally, spent of her anger, Daridar turned from the gate and started into the city.

In the smaller meeting room, in the palace, Gremble talked with the ogres and trolls, who were to be part of the aid in the protection of Neponia. He knew that the fairy folk, imps, and dragons, were holding their own meetings. He also knew that it had been decided that because of the Gorgamins, it would be best that the unicorns, sheep, and wolves, should not be sent. "Telalon is preparing the Neponian's for your arrival. As soon he has decided that they are ready, you will travel to that domain," he told them, letting his eyes make contact with each of them. The heads of those gathered, nodded with their understanding. "Because of the creatures that hunt the night, you will all be sharing the same quarters," he announced, and both races smiled, with shared glances and again, nodded their understanding. He looked to Zardan. "Has there been any words about the Milky Quartz that we will need?" he asked the leader of the trolls. Zardan shook his head.

"Coooooursel has gooooone to talk with the elves, foooor he has had thooooughts that might be oooof value." The other trolls nodded. "I have noooot heard oooof their decision yet." Gremble nodded.

"I am sure that we will hear soon," Gremble told all. He looked out over the gathered. "The Overseer has told me that there will be at least one squadron of Ventorians joining, and they too, will be quartered with us." There were surprised looks from them all. "We must all be ready for what is to come," he told them. Both races stood at the same time. The great roar from all, spoke the truth of their readiness.

———

Glornina came to the office, after her turn at the panel of talkers. Namson looked up as she entered and saw her expression of concentration. "What is it?" he asked as she sat in the chair facing him. She looked into his eyes.

"What if she is shielded and cannot answer?" Glornina asked. Namson looked to her in confusion.

"Are you talking of Daridar?" he asked, and she shook her head.

"Isabella," she told him. "What if she can hear our calls?" she asked. He looked to her.

"What do mean?" he asked quietly, already thinking he knew the answer.

"Both Gordon and Xanaporia have said she is a powerful magical talent. What if Isabella can hear our callings, but cannot answer?" she asked sitting forward and returning his look, intensely. "What if we start sending, to her, that Penelopy had had her sensing of her?" Namson began to allow a small grin to grow. "If we could get her to find this Daridar, and using whatever had caused Penelope's seeing, we could talk with her!" Namson didn't even realize that he was nodding.

"Do it," he told her softly. Glornina smiled as she raised from the chair and leaned over the desk. She kissed him, smiling as she pulled back.

"Yes, my Overseer," she told him, and turned to leave. He had already seen her eyes change, as she began to tell those of the panel to begin concentrating on Isabella.

Just outside of the building at the base of the mountain, sitting in chairs, Cartope and Neponities were talking with Telalon. Cartope already knew of the ogres, dragons, and fairy folk, but not of the imps. She was trying to help the Queen to understand the value of these races coming to Neponia.

"My Queen," she said. "I have seen the size, and power, of both dragons and ogres. They are much larger and stronger than even the Gorgamins." She leaned closer to Neponities. "We cannot rely on magic alone. These beasts will be able to attack as we cannot." Telalon frowned at her for her choice of words. The Queen saw the frown.

"Telalon, are Cartope's words true?" she asked quietly. The elf nodded.

"Yes, though they are not beasts," he told her. "Both races are quite intelligent, and are very powerful in physical strength, and many have magical talent. You must also add in the advantage of the dragons flaming!" Neponities right brow lifted slightly. Telalon continued. "The fairy folk are very good in communication, and they too possess magical power. Plus, they can go where others cannot, for their size," he said. "The imps, I have had little experience with, as there are none in Elandif, but from what I have seen while in the Realm, and know of their contribution to the war with the Dark Magic, they too will have great value." His voice had remained calm, but there was an assuring strength to his tone. She nodded slowly, as her eyes clouded with thought.

"I am not sure I want these strangers in Neponia," she said, almost softly.

"This will be only as long as needed for the defense of Neponia," Telalon said. "I am sure that there will be no desire for them to want to stay. They have their own lives in the Realm." Neponities stared at him, and he did not flinch from her look. Neponities took in a slow, deep, breath.

"They must not change the balance of life here," she told him. "They cannot even effect the Gorgamins, for they maintain a balance with the other creatures who could be trouble if allowed to multiply." Telalon smiled softly as he nodded.

"They are fully aware of that factor Queen Neponities," he answered her worries. "I assure you, they would only act in self defense, and they would be careful then," he added, hoping the Queen did not see the concern in his eyes. Again, Neponities stared and again, Telalon returned her look calmly.

"I will allow only a few of each, at first, and I will see what effect they have." She stood and left. Cartope sighed, looked to the elf, and shrugged. She stood and followed the Queen, as Telalon thought of how he was to inform the Overseer of this new development.

<hr />

Brandaro sat on the great couch. Both Morselia and Caratelia had taken refuge in their bedroom, fearing the rage of their Master. Brandaro's thoughts were racing through the plans he had made to return to the domain his father had raided, and the gains he had wanted from there. Porkligor and Rentaring, who had, quite some time ago, accidently learned of their leaders desires, continued their plotting to steal the bounty of that same raid. They both felt the nagging fear that Brandaro had somehow discovered their plans, through the dwarf they had frightened into working for them.

Isabella started to hear a new calling from those who had been seeking Daridar's attention, and hope began to build as she heard their plotting.

Daridar had begun her quest to control the females of Bandarson, ignoring the changed voices she had suddenly started to hear again. She was surprised, and proud, at the ease by which the women agreed to her plans.

Namson tried to keep track of all that was happening with the different races and was not pleased with Telalon's report. Melsikan thought of the woman he would never stop loving, and he continued to fear for her. Marcus and Penelopy continued their learning of each other, with a passion that was staggering, and very tiring, but not slowing them in the least.

In Pennes, Sophia plotted her revenge against all those of Zentler, she thought had turned against her, including her rebellious daughter.

CHAPTER FIVE

Isabella waited for Kris's return, listening to the words that were being sent to her, and she fought her frustrated desire to scream, because she could not answer them. The sound of a muffled step caused her to freeze with the fear that she had been found. She almost cried with her relief when Kris walked into the room. The girl placed the sack on the table and there was a very strange smile on her lips as she looked to Isabella.

"I have seen the one you say you must find, Daridar," she told Isabella and Isabella jumped from the chair she had been sitting in.

"Where," she screamed quietly. "I can use you, and her, to talk with those who can stop Brandaro." Kris reacted to Isabella's sudden outburst, by backing away from her. Her eyes narrowed suspiciously.

"Keep your voice down, and what is this talking you speak of?" she asked, her backing steps taking her further from Isabella. Isabella followed her retreat, her hands extended.

"No, please don't be afraid," she begged. "I told you I have magical powers, and it seems that when I touched you yesterday, I felt a jolt, and that contact allowed my cousin to see me."

"You felt a jolt too?" Kris asked quickly, her eyes opening wider. Isabella nodded and moved closer slowly.

"Yes, and that seems to have opened a connection between myself and my cousin in Zentler." She tried to keep her voice calm. "With the ability of this Daridar to talk with those of the Realm, I could talk with those there, using the connection with you, through Penelopy." Kris's eyes again narrowed with suspicion.

"What is this talking?" she asked again. Isabella sighed as she stopped and stood straight.

"It is magical communication, done with the mind," she told Kris. The girl still looked to her with doubt. "Just as we talk to each other now, with our voices, talkers can do the same over any distance, with their minds. The magic, that each of the magical domains possess, makes it so all they have to do is concentrate on the one they want to talk to. This Daridar can do it without even realizing how she can, I must find her, please." Isabella's voice turned to a begging tone. Kris stared at her as she mulled over what Isabella had just told her. Her eyes opened slightly.

"You say that the contact between us caused your cousin to see you?" she asked quietly, the suspicion easing from her eyes slightly. Isabella nodded rapidly. "I have never heard of this, not even with the travels in the castle. I'm not sure I understand," she said much softer. Isabella tried to smile and placed her hand on the necklace around her neck.

"I know you don't know what I mean, but I can tell you, that if it were not for this collar, and these bracelets, I could have already been able to be in contact with those who could destroy Brandaro." Kris stared at her again, and Isabella waited, her eyes begging.

"You are one of these talkers?' Kris finally asked. Isabella nodded slowly.

"I don't think that Brandaro knows that, but yes, I could talk with those of the Realm, and they would come and save not just me, but all those who suffer from Brandaro's cruel rule," Isabella told her. Kris's eyes carefully opened to normal as she stared at Isabella. She then held up her hand, indicating that Isabella should stay where she was. Kris moved to the other side of the table. She reached into the cabinet and took a glass and a bottle from it, never taking her eyes from Isabella's. Isabella did not move as she watched her new friend. Kris blew some of the dust from the glass and then poured it half full from the bottle. She took a deep drink from the glass and her eyes tried to water, as they looked to Isabella. Gaining control again, she took a smaller sip from the glass, still looking at Isabella. Kris pulled a chair back and sat slowly. Isabella started to move and Kris's hand quickly lifted, stopping her. "I swear to you," Isabella told her softly. "All that I have told you is the truth," she whispered. Kris slowly lowered her hand as she glanced at the necklace Isabella wore. She returned her eyes to Isabella's as she took another drink.

"You say that the contact with me, somehow allowed your cousin to see you?' she asked, almost calmly. Again Isabella nodded. "And, that if it were not for the necklace, you could talk with those you mentioned?" Again Isabella nodded. Kris again allowed her eyes to travel to the necklace and back. She again stared for some time. "If we could bring Daridar here, and you made contact with me, you could talk with those who could take Brandaro out of power?" Isabella nodded. Kris took another sip from the glass. She slowly placed the glass on the table and again, lifted her hand to Isabella. She slowly stood and reached for the cabinet without looking, retrieving another glass. She blew some of the dust from the glass as she sat again. She poured some from bottle into the glass and set it across the table from her, she had never taken her eyes from Isabella, and Isabella began to understand the real, and somewhat frightening power, that was Kris. She pointed at the chair, and Isabella slowly moved to the chair, and sat. She picked up the glass and took a sip. The fire in her throat caused tears to come to her eyes. Kris allowed a small grin to come to her lips. "Daridar would not come," she told Isabella as she took another sip from her glass. Isabella almost dropped the glass she held, and her tear filling eyes opened wide.

<hr />

"Why do you still worry about them Miss Sophia?" Dwayne asked her, still required to call her by that title, even though he shared her bed, occasionally. She glared at him and he dropped his eyes from hers.

"I will not be denied my revenge for their unwarranted attacks on me, especially that whore of a daughter," she proclaimed in a hiss. The girl who had been hired to clean and serve, sought refuge outside, claiming laundry duty. Dwayne glared from under his brows. If it were not for the fact that he had only been able to pilfer a small amount of the woman's gold and jewelry from her yet, he would teach her something about attacks. "Have you gotten the ones needed for that revenge yet?" Her voice holding nothing but contempt.

"Yes Miss Sophia, but they are seeking more money for what you ask," he told her, trying to keep his anger from his voice.

"What?" she screeched at him. "Do these sniveling low lives think they can demand from me? They should be grateful for what I offer them!"

"I understand that Miss Sophia, but if you want the extent of the revenge you demand, you may have to pay more for it," he told her. "I told you that from the beginning Miss Sophia," he managed in spite of the burning glare she aimed at him. He almost smiled as he thought that the money he spoke of, was for him, not the others'.

"It is your job to get me what I need, and you will do it, or you will find yourself with many more troubles than you want. The Mayor and Constable are very close friends you know," she hissed at him. He bowed and backed from the room. His anger tried to overcome his thinking, and it came close.

"Perhaps it is time for me to take what I have earned and get the hell out of here," he muttered as he headed for the shanty that held those he had been able to sort out of the recruits, for something other than what Miss Sophia wanted. He smiled as he thought of all those who had volunteered to deal with Miss Sophia's attitude. Miss Sophia had made many enemies since her arrival in Pennes, flashing her money and contempt around, as a sword! Even the Constable, the Mayor, and his wife, had secretly volunteered! He laughed out loud, as he neared the shanty.

Semotor looked to Tandetor, his cousin, and the one he had selected to lead the two squadrons of Ventorians, to Neponia. "You and your squadrons will be quartered with the ogres and trolls of the Realm," he told him and Tandetor nodded, with a small smile.

"I have already talked with Grable, who will command the ogres, and Boursel, the troll commander." Tandetor replied. "Do you yet know what dwellings we are to live in?" The General of the Armies of Ventoria shook his head.

"The Neponian's are being closed mouthed at this time. It seems they are worried about what the Dragons and ogres are going to want to eat, and how that will affect the balance of life on Neponia." Semotor growled. Tandetor looked surprised.

"Were they not told that the ogres are vegetarians?" he asked and Semotor shrugged with a grin of his own. "As far as the dragons, they're going to eat pretty much whatever they want, aren't they?" Semotor chuckled with his nod.

"The Overseer is talking with Telalon, the elfin elder on Neponia, who is trying to get the Queen to understand that none sent there, will endanger their balance of life," Semotor said. "In truth, they should be more concerned about what the trolls, and our squadrons are going to eat, then the dragons and ogres!" Tandetor laughed out loud with that statement.

"To say nothing of the imps," Tandetor added, and that got them both laughing. It was then that one of Semotor's aides entered, drawing their attention from the worries of the Neponian's.

"General Semotor," the aide stated. "Lord Calsorack is calling from Bendine. He says it is very important." Semotor and Tandetor both sobered immediately. Semotor went to the orb in the corner of his office. As soon as Calsorack's face appeared in the orb, Semotor saw a very frustrated look in his eyes.

"What is it Calsorack?" he asked and Calsorack almost managed a smile.

"Barsantorack is stirring up trouble again," Calsorack said in a very tired voice. "He's trying get me ousted as Bendine Governor, and get Tremarack to take my place, as Ruler!"

"Why would he be trying that?" Semotor's voice sounded almost as tired as Calsorack's. "Who is Tremarack?"

"Barsantorack is saying that Tremarack should be ruler, because he is a direct blood line descendent of Borack, and I am the descendent of a half blood." Anger slipped into Calsorack's voice now. "He also saying that the old ways are being destroyed, because the females no longer honored their husbands and are assuming an equals place."

"I bet Milserence is happy to hear that," Semotor said quietly. Calsorack's brows lifted as he shook his head, for everyone knew of Calsorack's wife's temper, and all the work she had done to improve all of the lives on Bendine Island. "What started this action from Barsantorack?" he asked in a normal tone.

"It would seem that Barsantorack applied for a high level position, and he was rejected," Calsorack said. "I wouldn't let that lazy, using, fat fool, into a position as street cleaner." Semotor nodded his agreement and smiled. "Barsantorack has been told that it is a decision that is to be made by the Ruler of Ventoria, but he says that Bendine should make its own rule and not be subject to the rest of Ventoria, as it was when Borack ruled. He is trying to stir up the male population into a physical attack if no other answer is offered them. He's making the point that Tremator has made him some kind of Chancellor, and he is to rule for Tremator! It also is a fact that Tremator was completely satisfied with the position he had before, and I am sorry he has let Barsantorack sway him, and endanger that. To say nothing of the fact that Simerence, Barsantorack's wife and Salsakor, Tremator's wife, are so mad they could spit Demons! I would like to see Tremator's punishment for this to be as minimal as can be."

"I shall be there within an hour," he told Calsorack. "I will talk with the Ruler and get his authorization first, and then we can do something about Barsantorack for once and all. The punishment of Tremarack is entirely your doing." Calsorack nodded.

"Thank you Semotor, I am really tired of that pain in the rear end of all Bendine!" Calsorack stated, and broke the connection. Semotor gave some simple directions to Tanderack, concerning the Ventorians who would be going to Neponia, and then started for the Rulers castle. The agreements that have been since the time Semirack had been named by Borack, to replace him, gave the Ventorian Ruler command over all of Ventoria, including Bendine. Considering that this was a dispute over the leadership of Bendine, which was that of a governor of the Ruler, required the Rulers authorization to be acted on. Semotor was determined to convince the Ruler that he should be as tired of Barsantorack, as Calsorack was!

It was early in the morning when Namson sent messengers to all the races of the Realm, to prepare four, of each race, to be ready to travel to Neponia. Glornina sat on the couch, in his office, and he could clearly see that something had captured her thoughts. As messengers returned, stating that the races were ready, he went to her, sitting beside her on the couch. "What have you been thinking so hard about?" he asked. She looked to him and he could see that her thoughts were not with him. "Glornina?" he asked again, and she came back to him.

"I'm missing something," she told him. He stared at her waiting for more information. "Something obvious that is alluding me," she continued.

"Are you still thinking of Isabella?" he asked her quietly and she frowned at him.

"Of course," her voice not hiding her impatience. He knew she was not impatient with him, but her own thoughts. Namson sighed.

"Remember what I told you about thinking too hard on one thing," he reminded her and she glared at him as the members of each race gathered in the rear yard of the palace. A voice from the orb saved Namson from the slow, agonizing death of Glornina's glare.

"Overseer," Telalon's voice called. Namson went to the orb and smiled at the happy face of the elf. "Neponities is ready to greet her guests, and I have been somewhat successful convincing her that the balance of life of her planet will not be affected by the races of the Realm, and Ventoria."

"That is good news Telalon, very good. I will send them immediately," Namson told him. The elf nodded.

"I might suggest that they come by size. That way, the Queen will be able to adjust, I hope." Namson grinned.

"Alright Telalon, by size they come," he told him and walked to the rear terrace. There, he began to arrange the order of travel, by size. The portal opened in the rear yard and the races began to file into it.

Neponities was surprised to find herself nervous, as the portal opened. Cartope stood to her right and Telalon, sitting in a chair, and Wenzorn, standing to his side, were on her left. First came the fairy folk, there were actually twelve of them. Next came the imps, again twelve in number. Then came the eagles and bats, though the bats were fighting to stay awake. Next were the trolls. Neponities and Cartope was surprised at the obvious strength of the short beings. The elves entered Neponia and they shared a smile with Telalon and Wenzorn. Then came the ogres and Neponities gasped at their size, but the following dragons, caused all but Telalon to exclaim at their size.

"By all the spirits!" Neponities cried out. Cartope had seen the dragons in flight when the Dark Domain had been attacked, but she had never seen them close up, and walking. She realized that they were larger than the fire dragons she had known. Her exclamation did not surprise anyone!

"Oh Shit," she said much louder than intended, and the all those of the Realm, laughed. Barsynia was just as shocked as the rest, but was still able to pass on her information to Somora.

———❦———

"I know that it has been horrible for you, and I cannot explain why, but I feel all will be right," Marcus told Penelopy quietly as he held her, just outside the kitchens door. She pulled her head from his shoulder and looked into his eyes. He saw the wanting to accept his words, in her eyes, but he also saw the fear she could not rid herself of, for Isabella. "I know that she will be fine and return to Melsikan. You know what, we all will be stronger for this," he added. She almost managed a smile as she nodded. As the last nod was given, her smile found its strength.

"I hope you are right, my husband." With those last two words, Penelope's smile grew. They kissed, and the loud, shocking sound of falling pots, pans, and who knew what else, came to them. "I had better go, I think," Penelopy said with an even bigger grin, after their lips had been forced apart from the noise. "I'm quite sure that Tarressa has struck again." They both chuckled as Penelopy turned and entered the kitchen, as they both heard the women in the kitchen cry out, in exasperation, the name of the young girl in question. Marcus turned to the business he had planned, a meeting with Melsikan. He heard Penelopy try to calm the women, and give support to the fifteen year old girl, who had the tendency to trip, or usually worse, if she tried talking and walking at the same time.

Marcus had not traveled very far when he was suddenly, and violently, slammed into the wall of a building. Marcus was a tall, strong young man, but as he fought against the grip that held him, he was unhappily unable to free himself from his assailant. He looked to the one who held him and was shocked to look into the eyes of Carl Bries, the older brother of Tarressa The Terrible, as she was called, unfortunately, many times to her face.

"Carl," Marcus yelled at him. "What the hell are you doing?" Marcus was even more surprised when he realized that Carl looked very much like a very tall troll, but as a human, he was short.

"I know that you, Melsikan, and Penelopy, are up to something," Carl yelled back in a voice that was much too deep for his size. Marcus again fought the hold of Carl and again, failed to free himself.

"Carl," Marcus tried to keep his voice calm, in spite of his anger that the smaller boy could hold him. "What the hell are you talking about?" Carl slammed him again into the building, hard.

"Don't play games with me Marcus," Carl growled and Marcus did not like the look in Carl's eyes. "I have been watching, and you have a lot of explaining to do," Carl's growl continued. "You know what has happened and why. You, Penelopy, and Melsikan, know why!" Carl's eyes got angrier. "Now you will tell me, or I am going to make you wish you had." Carl emphasized his words by slamming Marcus into the wall again. Marcus's mind began to race. He remembered when Carl was in school, how the older and bigger kids laughed and taunted him, for his size. He remembered when Tarressa started school and she was almost immediately sent home, to save the school, and the students, from her clumsiness. He remembered how Carl had fought any that condemned his sister, or any other person in his family. He remembered the stories of Carl's great grandfather and grandfather, as they were a very important part of the building of the reservoir that now fed Zentler the water they needed, but had been called names, and worse, for their size. All of this flashed through his mind in less than a second. He looked into the eyes of a young man, near his same age.

"All right Carl, I will tell you," Marcus said gently. Carl could not stop the look of surprise from his eyes, as a hand closed down on his shoulder. He winced from the power of the grip.

"Let him go." Melsikan's voice was calm, hushed, and deadly. "Or all that you threaten, will be wrought against you."

"No Melsikan," Marcus stated, looking to his new friend. "I swear to you, his family and he, have paid more than their share for the right to know." Melsikan glanced to him and then back to Carl.

"Let him go." His voice had lost the deadliness, but not the threat.

"Alright," Carl stated. Concession was in his voice, but not surrender. Carl slowly began to release Marcus and none made any move that would be construed threatening. "Release your grip," Carl said as he removed his hands from Marcus. Melsikan removed his hand and Carl rubbed his shoulder as he first looked to Marcus and then turned to face Melsikan. "You are not what you seem," he told Marcus's savior. "You all," Carl glanced at Marcus and back to Melsikan. His hushed voice came with a calm, and a knowledge; "have more than most, almost magical." His words caused an exchanged glance between Marcus and Melsikan. Silence and stares were shared between the three.

"What do you know?" Marcus finally asked as he moved next to Melsikan. Carl stood taller as he looked to the two.

"My sister has been telling me. Following those telling, I have been following you two, and Penelopy."

"Your sister?" Marcus asked with a very surprised tone. Carl nodded slowly.

"She says that she can hear talking, as though the people were standing beside her." Marcus and Melsikan glanced to each other. Carl's voice brought them back. "She says that Isabella lives and that those who would steal what is not theirs, are going to return." Melsikan suddenly remembered seeing Carl following Isabella, offering help when he could. He also remembered the friendship she said she felt for Carl.

"You love her," he said softly. Carl turned from the two and went to the wall. His fist clenched, and aimed to damage that what could not cry out from the pain, but when his hand reached the wall, his fingers were spread, and it touched softly.

"It don't matter," Carl's voice was now resigned. "She is in love with you, not me." Carl's head bowed. "Why would she want someone my size, when she could have you." There was no question in his voice, only pain. Melsikan came closer and again put his hand on Carl's shoulder. This time, with understanding.

"It is the size of your heart, not the size of your body, that gives your love strength," Melsikan told him. "She has told me of your attentions, and, that she feels you as a dear and important friend. One she could turn to in need." Carl spun to face Melsikan and for a second, his eyes flared with rage.

"I could not stop her taking!" he roared and, begged.

"Neither could I," Melsikan said softly; "and I have more power than you." The two young men shared a moment of truth between them, Marcus found interest in the toe of his shoe, as it dug slowly into the dirt.

"Can we get her back?" Carl asked quietly as tears formed in his eyes. Melsikan nodded and tried to smile.

"That is what many are now trying to do," he told Carl.

The more time that passed without finding the girl, the madder Brandaro got. Several of his guards, who were only reporting what their commanders had told them to, were killed with his rage. Telposar and Belidaria were having the times of their lives, and there were many that suffered for it. Many people now searched for the girl, not because Brandaro had ordered it, but to save themselves. Daridar had continued to ignore the voices she heard, for her goal was already in sight, when she realized that the voices were now trying to talk to the girl Brandaro sought. A new thought came to her and she liked the possibilities. She thought of her answer for the voices, as an evil, and greedy smile, came to her face.

Penelopy had managed to calm the women in the kitchen, and get the weeping Tarressa out of there. They stopped not far from the kitchen, in the shade of a tree. Penelope's arm around the very distraught girl.

"I know I am clumsy," Tarressa managed between her sobs. "I don't want to be! I want to be able to do as the others' do, without causing troubles," she continued as Penelopy tried to calm her. "But the voices are making it so much harder!" Penelopy jerked Tarressa from her embrace and looked at her with widened eyes.

"Voices?" Penelopy asked with a tightly controlled scream; "What voices?" she asked with a better control, now holding the girl at arm's length. Tarressa looked to her, her tears slowing and her eyes wide in fear.

"The voices I've been hearing in my head," she whispered. "They make it harder for me to concentrate," she added. A small smile came to her lips. "I know that you have had a sensing of her and they now talk to her and not that Daridar. I don't trust her at all!" Penelopy tried to talk and although her mouth worked, her words were not so cooperative. She stopped her efforts and quickly looked around. She saw that no one seemed interested in what they were about. Penelopy moved the girl farther from the possibility of being overheard. Stopping, she again took the girls shoulders in her hands and stared into her eyes intensely.

"Now, tell me everything you have heard, and why you don't trust Daridar." Tarressa stared back at her, fear coming to her eyes. Penelopy took a breath and slowly shook her head, and tried to smile. "Honey, it may be important. Please, tell me what you know." She spoke softly and Tarressa slowly began to relax, and, talk.

<hr />

"Why won't she come?" Isabella asked, both fear and anger in her question. "She has to come, I need her to come!" Isabella's voice was gaining volume, and panic. "I can't talk to the Realm without her!" Kris's hand shot out and clamped down on her hand.

"Don't start yelling," she said with anger of her own. "I don't need you to cause me to lose my home." Kris's eyes burned into Isabella's. "You can't trust Daridar!" Isabella's eyes opened wide. "What I've seen tells me that she has her own desires, and I truly feel that they would not be a benefit to anyone, but herself! Besides, you can talk to them through me, right?" Isabella had jumped from the power of the grip the girl had on her hand, and the jolt of her contact.

Penelopy suddenly jerked and stood tall. Tarressa looked at her in surprise and then smiled.

"Your sensing her now," she whispered. Penelopy nodded and looked into the girls eyes.

"Can you talk, or just hear?" she asked with a severity that frightened Terressa at first. She stared at Penelopy and then shrugged. "You have got to try," Penelopy told her. "You remember what Isabella looks like. Think of her, and try to talk to her with your mind, as though talking to her on the street, but only with your thoughts. Tell her I can see her." Tarressa nodded, and closed her eyes. The panel of talkers, as well as any that could talk, violently recoiled from the power of the voice that blasted into their minds. Penelopy watched the sight of Isabella and saw her suddenly twitch, and then smile.

"I can hear you Tarressa. I can hear you," Isabella said out loud, and Penelopy heard every word. Penelopy fought her scream.

"Tell her I heard her," Penelopy told Tarressa as Marcus, Melsikan, and Carl, came running towards them. "Is she safe? Is she alright? Where is she?" Penelopy was crying with her questions. Tarressa was crying as she passed Penelope's questions to Isabella. Penelopy saw the surprise on Isabella's face.

"You can hear me?' Isabella asked in a whisper, her eyes locked on Kris, who looked back with a look that she couldn't understand.

"Tell her yes, I can see and hear her," Penelopy cried to Tarressa. Marcus closed his hands on Penelope's shoulders, as Tarressa told Isabella, Penelope's words. Melsikan looked to both girls and he fought his tears of hope. Namson looked to Glornina's wide eyes, as they and many others listened to the one sided conversation of a previously unknown, and obviously, very, very, powerful talker.

———⚬⚬⚬———

Brandaro sat on his couch and thought. He had managed to mostly calm himself, but Morselia and Caratelia still kept their distance, unless he ordered them near. He was sure the girl knew what he wanted to know. His anger flashed through him again. His fingers played with the amulet around his neck, remembering the need to raid the domain that he and his father had, and soon, for the stones his father had gathered were almost all gone. He wanted more of them, and he wanted them to give him more power than the ones he had. He had learned of the Realm, the Plain, and the stones that could stop cast spells, from the two teachers who had been captured from a small, unknown domain, that the raiders had completely destroyed. It had taken but a little torture to get the man to tell him all about it. The woman, having watched what was done to the man, had quickly confirmed the man's words. Brandaro had then taken the woman and then gave her to his guards for their pleasure. The man, who screamed louder as he watched and listened to the rape of his wife, was killed. He didn't even think about the children of the two, who had somehow escaped.

He now worried that those of the Realm and Plain, would be trying to interfere with his plans. It had taken many years to find out where the Plain was supposed to be. That is why he had sent Porkligor to that town. He had hoped that they would find those of the domain called the Plain, but after he had had the eight captured females interrogated, rather painfully, he had learned that they did not know of it. That is why they now pleasured his male slaves. He had seen in the eyes of the girl, that she did know of the Realm, the Plain, and the stones, and he wanted her back! His thoughts were racing in circles when there came a gentle knock on the door, and one of the guards stepped cautiously into the room.

"Lord Brandaro, Pinsikar seeks an audience," the guard said, keeping his distance from the ruler. Brandaro could see the dwarf peeking around the guard. He beckoned him into the room and the guard quickly left.

"Lord Brandaro," Pinsikar stated as he walked carefully into the room. "I have something to tell that is of importance." Brandaro looked to the dwarf and his eyes narrowed slightly. Pinsikar stopped in front of Brandaro, just out of reach. "Porkligor and Rentaring are plotting something, and I fear it is against you," Pinsikar said, carefully watching his masters eyes. Brandaro looked at him for a moment before asking his one word question.

"What?" he asked simply. Pinsikar shuffled slightly before answering.

"I do not know what for sure," he said, not meeting Brandaro's eyes. "Pestikar, the spy I had following them, has not been heard from in days and I worry that he was caught by the two. He had confirmed my first suspicions about the two Captains plotting, before he disappeared." Brandaro stared at him, and he shuffled again. "Also, Daridar, my second daughter and mate of Pestikar has gone insane and attacked me when I asked about him." Brandaro smiled, for he had heard of Pinsikar's hurried return to the castle, and the female who chased him. "Master, I ask that you send guards and arrest Daridar, and force her to tell of Pestikar's location." Brandaro nodded slowly, and called for the guard at the door. The man entered the room carefully, getting no closer to the ruler than he had to. Brandaro looked to him, and an anger came to him as he saw the hesitation in the guards actions.

"Have the guards at the gate, who have seen the female dwarf called Daridar, chase Pinsikar, find that female and bring her to me," he ordered. "Tell Telposar to bring Porkligor and Rentaring to me, and not to be gentle about it." The guard quickly bowed and scurried for the door, after a quick and amused glance at Pinsikar. The soft leather sandals that Pinsikar wore, did not give the proper supporting sound to Pinsikar's stomp of embarrassment, and anger.

<hr />

"Make contact with Melsikan and have him bring those two here immediately!" Namson said to Glornina. She nodded and concentrated. Her eyes suddenly flew wide, and the five from Zentler appeared in the office.

"They were already preparing when I called to him," Glornina told her husband. Namson nodded and looked to the two young women and saw their smiles, and tears of happiness. He looked to Marcus and Melsikan and saw that they too had expressions of hope, and joy. He looked to the third young man and had to smile at the sickened look on the boys face. He spelled a calm to the lads stomach, and returned his eyes to the girls.

"Does she know where she is?" he asked Penelopy, but it was Tarressa who asked Isabella. Penelopy gave Isabella's reply.

"She says she has been rescued from Brandaro's clutches by a girl named Kris, and that girls contact with her, is causing this connection," Penelopy told all, and there were more and more coming into the office. "She says she is alright. She has not been hurt. Embarrassed, but not hurt. She is safe where she is." Penelopy suddenly gasped. "She says that the eight girls who had been taken with her have suffered greatly, and she doesn't even know if they still live." Namson took a step closer, and Penelopy held up her hand and stopped him. "She says that there has been a shielding collar and wrist bands placed on her, and she cannot use her powers. She says that only Brandaro, the ruler, and a monster, or his slave master, Besaline, can remove them." Namson looked to the other girl.

"I am going to try and use you to pin point her and spell her back here. Do you understand?" Tarressa nodded, passing Namson's words to Isabella as fast as she heard them and Penelopy suddenly smiled.

"Wait," she told Namson. "Isabella has an idea that she feels you should hear." Namson glanced at Glornina, who shrugged.

"Alright, what is her idea?" he asked. Penelopy nodded, not looking at anyone in the room. She then focused her eyes on the Overseer.

"She says that Kris feels, that this Daridar is not to be trusted, and Tarressa has to narrow her thoughts so that only she can hear her." Penelopy looked to Tarressa. "You said you didn't trust her," she whispered her words, and Tarressa blushed with her nod. "Can you concentrate and only talk to Isabella?" Tarressa looked at her and then around the room, which had by now, become quite crowded. She looked back to Penelopy and shrugged. "Would you try, please," Penelopy asked softly. Tarressa nodded and closed her eyes. There was a relieved sigh from all those in the room who suddenly didn't have Terressa's voice blaring in their heads.

"She's doing it," Glornina whispered to Penelopy. Penelopy nodded and looked to the girl whose shoulders she still held.

"You're doing it honey, tell Isabella that we have privacy." Tarressa nodded and passed on Penelope's words. Penelopy smiled and looked to Namson. "Here are her ideas."

————

Daridar, who had been listening to the one sided talking, suddenly couldn't hear what was being said, and she got mad. She knew that she could have used the hearing of these voices to gain favor, and power, from Brandaro, but now she suddenly couldn't hear them. She left the building she was in and headed for the castle of the Ruler of Bandarson, to get what value she could for her hearings.

————

As Namson listened to Isabella's idea, he spotted Coursel, Quansloe, Phemlon and Phelilon standing in the doorway of the office, and all four were grinning so wide, it just had to hurt!

————

Neponities was looking at all those who had come through the portal, as they now stood quietly waiting, stunned at the sizes, when a second portal opened and the representatives from Ventoria, who were the same size as the ogres, entered Neponia. Those of the Realm welcomed their friends as the wide eyed Neponian's stared, their mouths gaping. Neponities recovered from her shock first and stepped forward, followed by Cartope, drawing the attention of the visitors, and they quieted.

"Welcome all, to Neponia." Her voice carrying easily over the small glade. Traredonar and Ralsanac stepped to the sides of their mates. "I believe we have found quarters for all, but we are still unsure where you dragons can stay." Her voice, though seemingly strong, held a doubt that all could hear. Merlintile stepped forward and bowed to her.

"Our needs are simple Your Majesty. We will need only caves of some kind," he announced and Neponities nodded and then looked to Traredonar.

"Do we have caves that the dragons can use?" she asked and he bowed as he nodded.

"Yes My Lady, to the east, but they are more just caverns in the side of the cliffs," he told her rather softly. Merlintile smiled.

"That would be quite sufficient Your Majesty," he told the Queen. She looked to the dragon and nodded.

"Very well, Traredonar, arrange that the dragons are shown these caves. Ralsanac please show the others' where they are to be quartered." The two men bowed and beckoned to their assigned charges to follow. The bats followed the dragons, hoping to find a cave they could sleep in. Telalon beckoned to the elves to follow him.

The eagles took off and looked over the trees around the glen. The fairy folk and imps watched the separation of their friends and then looked to each other. Neponities saw their confusion. "What sort of housing will you small ones need?" she asked calmly. Miteen flew forward and hovered in front of her.

"We can comfortably live in the trees, as long as it is warm," he told her and she nodded.

"Alright, find what you need," she said, and waved her hand to the surrounding forest. "It stays quite warm here in the Center Section of Neponia," she told him. He bowed with a quick glance at her body, and returned to the fairy folk and imp group. They quickly separated into small packs and spread out in different directions. The Neponian's watched as the visitors were led to their billeting. "What have we gotten ourselves into?" Neponities asked Cartope quietly.

"I do not know My Queen, but whatever it is, we need them here," she replied just as quietly. Neponities sighed softly, with her lack of assuredness.

Brandaro could hear the screaming's of the female dwarf long before she was brought before him. The two guards entered the room carrying the dwarf between them, each holding an arm and leg. She was face down and madder than hell. Brandaro pointed the area in front of him and the guards simply dropped her there. As soon as Daridar hit the floor, she jumped back up and tried to attack the guards. One of them simply backhanded her, and she went flying. She lay quiet when she landed. Brandaro looked to Pinsikar.

"Check and see if she still lives," he told him quietly and dismissed the guards. Pinsikar went to Daridar and felt her chest for a heartbeat. He found one, and then let his hands wander over her. "Not now Pinsikar," Brandaro said with a chuckle. "You can have her later," he added. "Drag her here," he said and pointed to one of the female slaves. "Get some water and wake her," he told the slave. She bowed and went to the water container and dipped a large ladle full and brought it back. When Pinsikar dropped the arm he had used to drag Daridar back in front of his master, the slave poured the water onto her face. Daridar responded with a sputtering gasp and a yell. She tried to get to her feet and Brandaro put a holding spell on her. "I will let you stand when you learn the proper respect of where you are, and who you are before," Bandarson said with a definite tone of warning in his voice. She turned her head and glared at the Ruler.

"I have come to tell you of a traitor, and the danger that she is," she hissed at him and Brandaro looked to her strangely.

"What traitor?" he asked in a growl."

"I stand first," she demanded. Brandaro fought his anger and finally released her from the holding spell.

"Stand," he ordered. "Now what traitor?" he asked again as Daridar stood. She looked at him and then to Pinsikar and she sneered at him.

"Pestikar is dead because he could not give me the respect I was due," she told Pinsikar. "And if I could have caught you, you would have died as well!"

"What Traitor?" Brandaro roared. Daridar jumped with fear at the roar, and looked to the Ruler, her eyes showing that fear. Her eyes then smiled, with her lips.

"The one you lost, and now cannot find," she told him, and her smile grew.

"Where is she?" Brandaro growled and moved forward on the couch. Daridar tried to back from his movement, and the fear returned to her eyes.

"I know not for sure," she said quickly. "But she is not alone, and is being aided in her hiding," she said, the smile returning to her lips. "She now speaks with the voices, about you," she spat the last words at Brandaro. With a speed that Daridar would have not thought possible of a man Bandarson's size, he lunged forward, and his hand closed around her neck. He lifted her to be eye level as he stood. Panic now filled her widened eyes as her feet flailed, no longer connected to the floor.

"What voices?" he hissed dangerously. Daridar's small hands could not even come close to encircling the wrist of the ruler as she tried to hang on.

"The voices I can hear in my head," she told him. "Somehow, they have made it so I cannot hear them anymore, but I know they talk to her, and they plot against you." She was struggling to get her words out for the tightness of Brandaro's grip. Brandaro's eye bore into those of the struggling dwarf.

"What are these voices?" he hissed again.

"I know not master!" Daridar was panicking with thought that the ruler would strangle her. Bandarson shook her.

"Where do they come from?" he asked.

"I do not know, but they spoke of the girl, Isabella, and one called Penelopy, from Zentler," Daridar cried out as the tears of her terror ran down her cheeks. Brandaro looked to her with surprise, for that was the name of the town Porkligor had said he had attacked. He released the dwarf and Daridar landed on the floor, collapsing, and rubbing her neck, trying to find a normal breathing. Brandaro sat back down on the couch and looked to her.

"Tell me all you know," he told her almost quietly. "Do not leave out anything, or I will make you pay, very painfully!" Daridar had heard the many rumors of Brandaro's cruelties. With considerable fear, she began her telling. It took her almost an hour to tell all, including the death of Pestikar, and the reason for it. Brandaro listened and when she had finished, he still looked at her. She began to tremble under his stare. He suddenly signaled the guard at the door. The guard came to stand beside the dwarf still on the floor. "Put her in the cell near my quarters and make sure that Pinsikar has an extra key. Make sure there is a guard at the door of that cell constantly," he ordered. The guard nodded and grabbed Daridar by the back of her gown, and started to drag her from the room. Bandarson turned to Pinsikar. "You are free to use her as you want, but I advise you to take the guard with you or she will fulfill her threat concerning your death." Pinsikar nodded nervously and followed the now quiet Daridar. She struggled to regain her feet, as she was pulled from the room. Brandaro sat back and his thoughts began to race. There were two thoughts that overpowered all others'. How could the girl do this talking with the shielding necklace and wrist bands, and he had to hurry his attack plans. He strengthened the shielding around the castle, not realizing that the shielding only stopped those from the outside to magically attack the castle, but it didn't interfere with Isabella's connection with Penelopy. Neither could it stop Terressa'a powerful voice. It wasn't until much later that he wondered if any others could hear this talking, but by then, it was too late to be concerned about it.

Namson, Glornina, and several others', worked with Penelopy, Tarressa, Isabella, and the yet unknown Kris, to work out the plans they were all satisfied with. Namson had several times signaled to the four grinning in the doorway to wait, and they had all nodded their understanding. It had taken several hours to reach a final plan and then Isabella broke the connection with a promise of when she would be in contact again. Another hour went by as those of the Realm began the initiation of their part of the plan. The most important part of which was that all talkers would keep all communications in a tight beam, to only the one they wanted to talk with. Orbs would be used more often, to keep their talking's from being heard by those who should not hear them. Messages were sent to all the domains and Neponia. Leaders were assigned to head up the many different parts of the plan. Finally, Namson called the troll, Keeper, and two elves, to him.

"The girl, Isabella, is quite something," Phemlon said with a grin, as he settled into a chair. "To have gone through all that she has, and still have the calm of planning." Namson grinned and nodded, with lifted brows.

"Yes, it would definitely seem so," he said and then looked to each before him. "Alright, what is causing your grinning?" he asked. Phemlon looked to the other three and they nodded that he should be the one to speak for them.

"Coursel has solved the Milky Quartz sizing problem," he stated and Namson's brows went higher as he looked to the troll. "Based on what Wenzorn has told us of the Power Stones the bandits have, and the deductions made from the assault on Zentler, we have determined that the basic magical talents of the bandits cannot be that high," Phemlon continued. "With the layering concept Coursel has found, we only need to make a few experiments with stronger magical powers, to find the proper thickness to make the amulets that will stop any of the bandits spells."

Namson looked to the four and he wore a confused expression.

"Layering?" he asked. The four before him nodded and their smiles returned.

"The Milky Quartz has a straight grain texture," Coursel said. "By cutting the stoooone thinly and layering the cut stoooones, crooooosing the grains, it multiplies the stoooones ability to absooooorbe the cast spells."

"We only have to figure out how many layers are needed," Phemlon added. Namson again looked from one to the next, and then began to nod. "We will need to use the power stone you have, to experiment with." Phemlon's voice contained a small amount of worry in it.

"Recruit whoever you can find free, and let me know when you will need the stone," he told them with a grin of his own. They nodded and rose from their seats. Coursel stopped at the door and turned back to Namson.

"Doooo noooot foooorget the value of the fairy folk, in yoooour plans," he said quietly, and left the office. Namson looked at the spot the troll had occupied. He finally started to see what the troll had meant. He called several people back to the office and presented a small variation to the original plan. There were many smiling people who left that office. They quickly spread the new ideas to the proper races.

Kris looked at Isabella as the girl rubbed her temples. "You could talk with them?" she asked in a whisper. Isabella smiled and let her hands drop to her lap as she returned Kris's look.

"Yes and we have formed a plan to stop Brandaro from any more of his cruelties," she told her. Kris still held a expression that Isabella could not figure out.

"I was touching you, but I felt nothing, nor heard anything of any of your voices," Kris said still whispering. Isabella began to worry about how Kris was reacting to what had happened. Kris refilled the glass before her. She took the glass in one hand and picked up the bag of food with the other, as she rose from the table. She went to the fire pit and began to make a fire. Isabella followed, and her fear was growing.

"What's wrong Kris?" she asked as she neared the girl. Kris didn't answer her. Isabella came around and knelt down, looking into Kris's eyes. "What's wrong?" she whispered. Kris looked to her and then back to the fire that had caught quickly. "Kris?" Isabella asked again. Again Kris looked to her.

"What's to happen to me when your friends come and destroy Bandarson?" Kris asked quietly. Isabella almost laughed out loud with relief.

"Whatever you want to happen," Isabella told her, as Kris stared into her eyes. Isabella nodded her head slowly. "You could even come to Zentler with me, if you wanted," she told the girl, and started to reach for her. Kris jerked back with a smile.

"Remember what happens when we touch," she almost giggled, and then sobered quickly. A few moments of silence passed. "Could I really?" she asked in a whisper. Isabella grinned and nodded rapidly.

"Yes, you surely can, and I know that you would love it there," she told her. Kris looked to her and a grin tried to take over the corners of her mouth.

"Can you tell me about this Zentler of yours?" she asked as she started to get a pan ready for the food she had brought. Isabella laughed and began to tell Kris all that she could of Zentler, as Kris started to cook their breakfast.

———

The castle guard, Mastone, did not want to admit that he was too afraid to return to the castle and face the wrath of Brandaro. That was why he now walked the small knoll that was outside and very far from the rear of the castle walls. Unexpectedly, the feint smell of cooking meat came to him. He stopped and looked around. He saw no smoke of a cook fire, and there should not have been anyone cooking here anyway. He moved forward and found the smell growing stronger. He followed the scent and came to a large patch of tall, thick, bushes. He parted them and saw a hole in the ground, about two feet in diameter. He crawled to the hole and looked down. His surprise almost caused him to lose his grip and fall into the hole. There, forty feet below him, were two girls sitting next to a fire, and one he recognized immediately. He had been the one to lock her in that cell. He backed from the hole and ran for the rear castle gate.

CHAPTER SIX

Barsantorack was truly enjoying himself. He had easily convinced that fool Tremarack, to follow his plotting, without even letting him know what his true reasons were. Although he had not yet wrestled Calsorack from the palace, he had a surprisingly large portion of Bendine listening to him with what he dreamed to be respect. He simply ignored the mutterings of his wife and children. He was not going to let anyone deflate his bubble of happiness. Then word came that Semotor had come to Bendine, and he had brought a squadron of soldiers with him, and that they had gone directly to the palace. This was the part that Barsantorack had been waiting for. He sent runners to pass the word that Bendine was now under attack from the rest of Ventoria, and they intended to drive all of Bendine to their knees, to rule them as slaves! He also added that Calsorack was going to help them do it! A large crowd of angry Bendine males quickly began to form in front of the palace gates. Another crowd began to form, to the side of the first, and had already seen the squadron of soldiers arrive, were calling the angry males in front of the gate, fools for following Barsantorack's stupidity. Barsantorack tried to prance to the head of the rebel rousers, but his bulk prevented it. He stopped, facing the gate, in front of those he had fooled.

"Calsorack, Semotor," he called, trying to roar, and failing, for his voice was too high pitched. "Bring forth your army of slave masters, and face the true residents of Bendine!" The gate opened and Calsorack and Semotor marched out. Behind them came the squadron of soldiers, forming a line behind the two, and they were all Bendine. Not one of the soldiers carried a weapon. A murmur spread through the rebels and Barsantorack didn't like what he heard. "Now try and impress us with the army you brought Semoter!" Barsantorack tried to bluff. Semotor and Calsorack smiled.

"This is the squadron I have brought Barsantorack," Semotor told him, and the now quiet crowd behind the fat one. "You have tried to fool these people of Bendine with your lies and greed. I am here to show the truth." The crowd that had already seen the landing squadron, started to laugh at those who would rebel with Barsantorack. Many of those, now looked at Barsantorack with distrust and anger.

"What is this about Barsantorack?" a voice called from the rebels. Barsantorack began to feel worry.

"They are trying to fool you, not I." Barsantorack tried to continue his bluff. "Have not all I told you about the turning from the true ways of Bendine, been the truth?" Some of the crowd nodded. "Have I not stood with you in our efforts to regain the true ways of Bendine?" Fewer heads nodded, as talk was begun in the crowd. Some even turned and left. "We have to stand together, behind the true blood descendant of Borack, to regain our world!" Barsantorack continued.

"Then where is this true blood leader?" a voice called from the outer crowd. The angry face of Barsantorack turned to where the voice had come.

"I am Tremarack's Chancellor! That is all that is needed!" Barsantorack cried out and, most heard the desperation in his voice. More of the would be rebels left. Barsantorack began to panic, and sweat. He had planned to well, too long, for his revenge. He had to take Calsorack down! "Do not leave!" he screamed at the deserters. "We can regain our proper rule when Calsorack is replaced by Tremarack, and me!" In the surrounding crowd, which had gotten much larger, laughter started again slowly, but it quickly spread. As the volume of that laughter grew, more and more of Barsantorack's would be followers began to leave him. He grabbed two of the smaller ones near him. "Are you cowards to run away and hide from your true Ruler?" he screamed at them, trying to throw them to the ground. They fought from his grip with little difficulty. One punched him in his face, hard.

"You have lied to us again Barsantorack and we will not listen to you anymore," the one who had thrown the punch yelled. Barsantorack held the side of his face as the laughter grew louder still. His eyes were wide, and his dreams were flying from him as the last of his followers walked from him. His hand fell to his side as he screamed at all.

"You are all cowards and I will teach you the proper respect when I rule Bendine!" His yelled words spread out over the witnesses. Their laughter died immediately, and their angry eyes settled on him.

"You will never rule anything Barsantorack," a voice called out, and the mob surged towards him. His eyes were now wide with fear, instead of anger. He backed from the closing mob until Calsorack's and Semotor's hands landed on his shoulders. Barsantorack looked back and forth between them.

"You have got to protect me!" he screamed at them, and they smiled.

"Why?" Calsorack asked calmly, as the mob drew nearer. Barsantorack's eyes were now showing the panic that was beginning to consume him completely. Semotor and Calsorack turned around and each took one of Barsantorack's flabby arms. They led him, walking him backwards, through the line of soldiers and through the gate. The soldiers closed their ranks behind them, forming a line that the oncoming mob stopped short of. The mob yelled their desire that Barsantorack be turned over to them. Some yelling very graphic descriptions of what they wanted to do to the fat one, but they never challenged the line of soldiers. After several minutes, Semotor reappeared and raised his hands for silence. It was slow in coming, but finally the angry mob looked to him in silence.

"Barsantorack will be punished by the laws of Ventoria," he told them, and there were several that stated clearly that they would rather handle that job themselves. "You will all now return to what you were about before this happened, and leave this matter to the authorities," Semotor told them and the troops took several steps forward. Not wanting to battle with the well trained soldiers, the mob broke up and returned to their lives.

That was not the last time any of them saw Barsantorack. He was tried and convicted for his rebellious ways, and sentenced to work in the mines. But because of his bulk, he was assigned to work in the offices. With that connection to information, he was able to build a sizable number of ways to blackmail and lie. Each time bettering his position. He also managed to build a large following among the others who had been sent to the mines for the crimes they had committed against the Ventorian society.

No one had blamed Barsantorack's family. In fact, Barsantorack's children rose in favor of the Governor, and Semotor, and became a large assent to all of Ventoria! Tremarack was allowed to return to his position as supervisor of the ore docks, but none that worked those docks would work for him. So, in shame, he went to work in a menial lookout position, on the southern coast and far from Bendine City. What surprised most, was that Salsakor, his wife, stayed with him. Their son and daughter, Tramerack and Palserence, were given the house in the city, but Salsakor went with her husband, to the outpost.

Brandaro received the much subdued Porkligor and Rentaring at the same time the guard brought word of the finding of the girl Bandaro had been seeking. He instructed four guards to take the two, badly beaten captains. to the inquisitors, to find out what they were plotting, and had the guard brought to him.

"Where is she?" Brandaro demanded after the guard bowed his respects. The guard straightened and smiled with a knitted brow.

"In a deep cavern, behind the castle," the guard told him. Bandaro looked to him waiting for more. When the guard didn't continue, Brandaro lost his temper.

"Why didn't you capture her and bring her?" he roared at the now fearful guard before him. Mastone swallowed hard.

"The only entrance I could see was a small hole in the ground and it was at least a forty foot drop." Mastone almost whispered. Bandaro tried to control his anger.

"Take a dozen soldiers, find an entrance and bring her to me!" he ordered very loudly. Mastone bowed several times as he scurried from the room. Brandaro took several calming breaths and then called for his Captain of the Guards, and the Commander of the troops who had been selected for the raid on the Domain with the stones he sought. He sensed his time was growing short.

Sophia was not prepared for the surprise Dwayne and his small band had planned for her. They dragged her from her bed a couple of hours before sunup. Dwayne used a leather strap, applied to bared sections of her anatomy, to convince her to tell him where the key to the locked door of the chamber, that held all the money, gold, and jewels, she had stashed away. She wept for her pain, her shame, and her rage, at his actions. She screamed curses and threats of reprisal for what he had done, and the entire band laughed at her. They bound her, the bared, bruised, and red, sections of her body still exposed, and quickly transferred the loot from the chamber to a waiting covered cart. Dwayne, when finished with his looting, walked to her with an evil grin on his lips. His eyes traveled the uncovered parts of her body and then returned to her eyes.

"One final thing before I leave you Miss Sophia," he told her softly. She looked passed him and saw the men of the band loosening their pants, and approaching her. Her eyes widened, and she screamed her denial of what they were about to do with her. Dwayne laughed at her screams as one by one, the men of the band sadistically used her. When they had finished and left, laughing at her, Dwayne knelt down and grabbed her hair, pulling her face close. "Now how high and mighty do you feel?" he hissed his question at her, and threw her down to the ground. His laughter covered her sobbing as he too went to the cart. They drove off as the sun cleared the horizon. It took her several hours to get herself loose from the bindings, and find clothes to wear. She then limped to the mayor's office, searching for justice for what had happened to her. Her troubles worsened when the mayor refused to respond to the horrors she had experienced. In fact, he flat told her that as she was now a pauper, and unable to maintain the rent on the house she had taken, she had to leave Pennes, and never return. The Constable and several of his officers arrived and escorted her back to her house. They helped her pack a simple back pack, of clothes and food, and escorted her to the southern end of town and pointed.

"Go back to where you came from, if they will have you," he ordered. "Do not ever return, or you will be jailed, and forgotten!" he added with a glare. Rage came to her eyes.

"When I do return, I will not be the one jailed," she swore to him. "You will be lucky if I let you live!" she yelled, and turned south. The Constable laughed until she could no longer hear him. It took her several days before she came to Olistown. She tried to get help from the people there, but it did not take long until they had had enough of her attitude, and sent her on down the road. It took her several months to get back to Zentler, as she had been jailed, as a vagrant, and a disturber of the peace, in Mastilar, the large town between Olistown, and the mountains. When she did finally reach Zentler, no one recognized her for her less arrogant attitude, or the wearing her traveling experiences had caused her appearance. They did not welcome her when they finally figured out who she was, except for one. He surprised everyone with his acceptance of her. The lower part of his left leg had been cut from him as he had worked to help all of Zentler. No one remembered the attraction the two had had, before she turned to greed, and had gone for the banker who was becoming rich. He remembered, and took her back into the heart that had never given her away. Randy had loved her since they were very young, and that love was rekindled when he saw her vulnerability with her return, as the town wanted to turn on her.

"We are both less than what we were, but together, we are more than most." He had told her. She looked to his shortened leg, his crutch, his eyes, and went into his arms. They surprised everyone again, when they wed and moved into Randy's small shack, a half mile west of town. There they found the truth of a happy life for the first time for each. He was the one that taught her the value of the magical world around them, and her daughters role in it. In time, Penelopy even learned to be proud of her mother.

———

Dwayne and his small band did not keep their spoils long, for the first town they came to, they stayed drunk for several days. In that time, their mouths spoke words of their riches, and the means by which them came by them. Shortly after they had moved on towards the north, they were set upon by those of the area who were just like them, and they lost their ill gotten gains, and their lives.

———

Neponities, followed closely by Traredonar, walked into the small field that fronted the house that was the quarters of Telalon, and the other elves from the Realm, as Cartope and Ralsanac entered from the opposite side. They were surprised to find the leaders of the different races gathered as they discussed the defenses of Neponia. Each of the races had explored all of the area around Capital city, as well as the city itself. Those gathered, gave the proper bow of respect to the Queen, and she returned the bow to them.

"I have been monitoring the effect of those of the Realm and Ventoria, on our land, and I can see no reason not to allow the remainder of their kinds, to come to Neponia," she announced and there was a small cheer given by all of the Realm and Ventoria. She looked to Telalon. "Have you decided on what defenses are needed to repel the attackers?" she asked as Cartope arrived at her side. Telalon nodded.

"Yes your Majesty," Telalon told her from his chair. "We have come to a basic decision. With the added forces, we feel that our success, although not easy, will be complete. Of course, that is at this time a guess, as we do not know for sure the number that will attack, or power level of those attackers. With the work being done in the Realm on the Milk Stones and the establishing contact with Isabella, one of the girls taken in the raid of Zentler, who has magical talent, we think we have an excellent chance." Neponities nodded, allowing a smile to come to her face.

"Please, tell me of these plans," she asked quietly, as she sat in the chair that had been brought her. Telalon and many of those of the Realm nodded, and they in turns, began to tell of their plans. It did not take long for the Queen, and the others' of Neponia, to see the real value of those from the Realm. Barsynia dutifully passed on those plans to her King.

Namson sat in his office and his thoughts worked from one point to the next, as he tried to see any flaws with the plans being made. He had just spelled the Power Stone to Phemlon, for the test of the Milky Crystals, and although he was sure of the security of the Realm, he had placed many around the experiment area, for added protection. He found that he couldn't just sit. He had to get up and move, for there was something that did not seem right, and he couldn't quite figure out what it was. He left the office, turning towards the rear terrace, planning to walk among the many gardens, trees, and fountains, that Glornina had arranged since her time as his wife. When he stepped out onto the terrace he was very surprised to see Zachia, Emma, and their two children, Mike and Mergania, as well as Glorian and her three, Heather, Telkor and Belkor, from the Canyon, and Michele and her two, Mearlanor and Dafnorian, from Calisonnos. They were all playing tag, and laughing as only loving families could. Zachia spotted him first and tried to beckon him to join. Namson simply held up his hand, with a slow shaking of his head, and sat down on one of the loungers. Emma had witnessed the exchange, and looked to the Overseers three children. She nodded to them, with a tilt of her head, towards the Overseer. Zachia, Glorian and Michele walked to the terrace, and their father. Zachia looked to his father and saw that something troubled him.

"What is it Papa?" he asked quietly. Namson looked to him and then the other two, in turn. He finally shrugged and tried to smile.

"I don't know for sure, but I feel as though something is not right with what we plan," he said more to himself then to them. The three exchanged concerned glances.

"What could be wrong Papa?" Glorian asked. "You have planned well, and we all, and those of all domains, think so." Again, Namson tried to smile at her.

"Overseer," Pelkraen startled them all, even though he had spoken softly. "Telalon calls from Neponia."

"Thank you Pelkraen." Namson said as he rose from the lounger. He nodded to his children and entered the Palace. He reached his office, and quickly went to the orb. "Yes Telalon, what is it?" Namson asked the elves face that waited.

"The Queen has given her permission to bring the rest to Neponia," Telalon told him. "Have you any news of the Milky Crystals yet?"

"I shall have the rest ready for travel this afternoon." Namson said. "Phemlon and the others are experimenting as we speak. As soon as we learn the results, I will let you all know." Telalon nodded.

"I shall prepare for their arrival." The elf broke the connection as Namson stared at the orb. A thought trying to break free from the clouding that hid it.

"What if he attacks before they are ready?" Michele's voice caused Namson to jump. The suddenly freed thought tore through his mind as he turned to his youngest daughter, his eyes widening.

"That's what is wrong," he told her. "I had not thought that he might attack before we can ready Neponia for him!" He had almost achieved a smile when Phemlon and Phelilon entered the office, both grinning widely. Namson looked to them and his hopes grew with their grins.

"It is amazing what that troll knows," Phemlon said as he held out the Power Stone. Namson took it and spelled it back to its chamber. "The very first test was all that was needed. Coursel had already prepared a very correct stone for the test, and it worked perfectly." Phelilon was nodding his agreement as Glornina entered the office.

"They used my power, with the Power Stone, for the test, and the Milky Quartz amulet Coursel had designed, worked perfectly," she told Namson as she came to him. Namson was grinning as he kissed her gently. He turned to Phemlon.

"How soon can the amulets be ready?" he asked.

"There will be stoooones enough to send with the reinfoooorcements to Nepoooonia," Coursel's voice boomed as he entered the office. He almost managed a blush with his next words. "I had thooooughts that the stoooone I had designed woooould be what we needed, and already had started toooo prooooduce them," he told all in the room, and wide grins answered him.

"Excellent," Namson said much too loudly. "Send messengers to notify all the races to prepare the remainder for travel to Neponia."

"I have already taken the liberty to do so Overseer," Pelkraen said from the doorway, not seeing the slowly passing Baldor.

"Papa," Michele said quietly. Namson looked to her and he saw something in her eyes, he was sure he was not going to like. "I have talked with Crendoran and we are going to Neponia, to lead our forces there." Her voice was calm, but there was no questions allowed with her statement. Silence came to the room. Glornina stepped closer to her youngest. There were no words spoken between mother and daughter. For minutes, all looked between the two as Namson's thoughts raced. None knew the dragons as Michele did. None knew the fairy folk as well as Michele. The youngest, and smallest of his children had, in her own way, made herself a center for all the races, for they all liked and trusted her as none other. Glornina took her daughter into her embrace as Crendoran appeared in the office. Namson was again amazed at the power of the young man. Unlike his grandfather, Crendosa, Crendoran was not of a delicate build. He was more like his father, Vandora. Broad of shoulder, and strong of arm. Namson knew that Crendoran's magical power, though not his daughters strength, was still quite high. He came to his wife and placed his arm around her as Glornina released her embrace, but still held her hands on her daughters arms. She looked to Crendoran and then back to Michele.

"Be careful my love," Glornina said softly, and then looked to the man who was her son-in-law. "Guard her well," she told him. He smiled with his slight nod. Glornina turned to her husband. "I will prepare them for Neponia," she said simply, and led the two to the couch and began to instruct them of what they faced, especially the dress code of the Neponian's. Namson turned to Coursel.

"When can the stones be ready?" he asked. Coursel smiled.

"There will be enoooough for oooour foooorces, when they leave. There will be enoooough for the Nepooooonian's very quickly!" The troll stated with the swelled chest of his kind, as both elves nodded their agreement. Namson nodded. So did Baldor as he snuck off to tell this news to Somora.

"Get them gathered, for our forces will leave shortly." Coursel nodded and hurried from the office, as many of the races began to gather in the back yard of the Palace.

Mastone had left one of the guards at the hole, to watch the two girls, as he led the others in a circle search for the entrance. Unfortunately, he had not left the smartest, or the cleanest of the soldiers. It took him several hours until he stumbled onto the secret door, almost completely unrecognizable. He had known that the entrance would be designed to look like anything but what it was, and that was what he looked for. At the same time that Mastone began to carefully pushed open the small door, the guard at the hole, unable to control himself, began to drool at the two pretty girls below him, and the smell of the food they ate. Isabella's head came up slowly and she looked to Kris with eyes showing surprise.

"What is it?" Kris asked softly. Isabella looked at her for several moments, as the guards drool began its decent to them.

"Daridar is calling for help," Isabella said quietly. "She has been found out, and Brandaro has put her in a cell, allowing Pinsikar use of her," she continued. Isabella's eyes opened wider. "She is calling to me! She says she will do whatever I say, but please save her." Isabella stood and looked to Kris. "She is in the same cell as I was." The guards drool landed in the remainder of the fire and sizzled loudly. Both girls looked up, and both saw the guard before he could pull his head back from their sight.

"Shit," Kris said as the distant echoing sounds of a large amount of metal clanging down a shaft came to them. "Oh, deep shit!" Kris shouted. "They have found the entrance! Come," she screamed and grabbed Isabella's wrist. She pulled Isabella towards the back of the cavern as Penelopy sat up and cried out.

"What about Daridar, we can't just leave her?" Isabella shouted as Kris pulled her.

"There's another way to that cell, but first we save ourselves," Kris yelled at her and pulled Isabella into an opening that she had just opened in the rear wall. "You do not want to know what Brandaro would do to us if we're caught. Come on," she told Isabella as the stone of the wall closed behind them.

"Penelopy," Isabella whispered as she held Kris's hand, following her down the dark tunnel. "If you can hear me, tell someone to tight beam a message to Daridar, and tell her I'm coming. She has to stay strong until I can get there." Penelopy told Tarressa to tell her that she had heard, as she pulled the clumsy girl behind her, racing for the Mayor's office. Once told of what Penelope had been told, Gordon sent the two on to the Overseer's office.

<hr />

"You all have your assignments, we will attack in minutes!" Brandaro told those gathered around him. "Get everyone ready," he growled as his huge fist slammed down on the table, causing all the mugs to jump and spill. Those of the meeting, fled to their duties, except Telposar and Belidaria. They grinned.

<hr />

Penelopy burst into the Overseers office, and all eyes turned to her. "Isabella is in danger and flees. She says that someone must tight beam a message to Daridar that she will be there soon to rescue her!" she screamed to the full room. There were exchanged looks, and Glornina called to Aaralyn, the one to make first contact with Daridar.

⸻

The guard laughed as Pinsikar tried to take Daridar. She fought with a strength the male could not match. "Here little thing," the guard said as he swept Pinsikar from the female. "Let me show you how to do it!" He grabbed the naked dwarf and forced her to the wooden bed. She suddenly twisted her head and clamped her teeth on the guards wrist, her teeth sinking deeply into the flesh of the guard, as her knee came up, with all the strength she had, between his legs. The guard let out two very loud screams as a result of her efforts, and released her. That was all she needed. She kicked Pinsikar in the same region she had kneed the guard, and fled through the door of the cell that had been left open. Naked and not caring, she fled down the hallway. The message from Aaralyn came as she was donning the simple gown she had taken from the first dwarf female she had come to, and incapacitated. She smiled as she thought her reply.

"I'm not in the cell anymore, and I will rescue her!" she told Aaralyn, and laughed out loud, as she made her way deeper into the castle. Because of the lopsided shield Brandaro had placed and had reinforced since Daridar's telling of the talking, Aaralyn never heard her.

CHAPTER SEVEN

Two portals opened on the edge of the small glen, and the remaining forces of the Realm came from one, and the troops of Ventoria came from the other. One ogre carried a rather large box. As soon as the portal closed, those of the Realm and Ventoria gathered around the ogre. He placed the box on the ground and began to hand out the amulets the box contained. Neponities watched these actions, and concern came to her as she did not see any Neponian's receiving amulets. Then she saw the girl, small in size, but somehow, Neponities saw the strength the girl commanded.

"Your Majesty," Michele said softly, as she held the amulet so it could be seen. "This amulet will stop any spells the bandits might invoke." Neponities hesitated only slightly before she bent, lifting her hair, to receive the amulet Michele placed around her neck. As she stood straight again, she noticed the small one before her, did not wear an amulet. She looked to the girls eyes.

"You do not need the amulet?" she asked softly. Michele blushed slightly, but did not take her eyes from the

Queen, as she slowly shook her head. Neponities right brow lifted slightly as she looked to those of the Realm and Ventoria, the male with the girl, who wore an amulet, and then to the girl herself. "You are the Overseers daughter," she said more than asked, and Michele nodded once.

"My name is Michele," she told the Queen. "This is my husband, and the father of my children, Crendoran." She indicated the man with her. Crendoran bowed, fighting his eyes from the Queens body. The Queen looked surprised.

"Someone so young, and, small? You have children?" she asked. Michele smiled and nodded.

"Two girls, Mearlanor, Dafnorian," she said with pride. The Queen looked her up and down and then smiled.

"You bear another, although just starting, and it is a boy," The Queen said softly. Michele's eyes sprang wide and glanced to Crendoran. He shrugged, wearing a look that caused the Queen to laugh out loud.

———❦———

"I've been thinking about how we should approach Bandarson," Glornina announced to all of the room, and heads turned to her. Namson smiled at her.

"So have I, but please, tell me your thoughts," he told her.

"We should attack as soon as possible!" Zachia stated with a furiousness that sent a chill up Namson's back.

"If we do that, we put Isabella in greater danger, as well as any others who are captured there," Glorian told her older brother, with a patronizing tone.

"Let's hear what your mother has to say first," Namson's voice interrupting the beginning battle between his two oldest. "Then we will decide," he added in a more gentle tone. Glornina smiled at her son and daughter, and then looked to her husband.

"I agree we must attack soon, but we know nothing of what is there, or where to go." She glanced to Penelopy and Tarressa. Namson nodded his head slightly and waited, as a grin pulled at the corners of his mouth. "We must find out all we can from Isabella and this Kris," she told them calmly. Both nodded and Tarressa closed her eyes and began to question Isabella, with Penelopy feeding her the questions to ask. Zachia sighed, already knowing his plan was outvoted. Namson looked into the eyes of Calteen, who had come with the remainder of the fairy folk going to Neponia.

"Yes, we are going to attack soon, but we are going to start slowly, with a dozen fairy folk." Calteen's brows lifted slightly as he nodded, and a smile came to his face. Salear looked from her husband's eyes, to the Overseers, and she started to worry of what they both seemed to understand, and she did not. Baldor passed this news to Somora.

⸺⸻⸺

Isabella tried to question Kris about the layout of the city around them, as the girl dragged her from one tunnel to the next. Suddenly, Kris stopped pulling her wrist, and slapped her other hand over Isabella's mouth. "You must be quiet now," she hissed into Isabella's ear. "We are nearing Brandaro's quarters and those two parsha's of his, can hear a mouse tip toeing through a wall." There was just enough light in the tunnel they traveled, that Isabella could clearly see the intensity of Kris's eyes. She nodded and lifted Kris's hand slightly and whispered to Penelopy that she would talk later, when it was safer.

⸺⸻⸺

Daridar wasn't really very sure what she was looking for until she ran into it, literally. She had been traveling at a faster than trot speed, constantly checking behind her for pursuit. She glanced over her shoulder as she neared a corner. As she planted her foot to make the corner, she turned her eyes back to the front, and into the ample bosom of Besaline, the slave master, who was traveling at a fair rate of speed herself. She was trying to get as far from Brandaro as she could. The two collided. Although Besaline far outweighed the dwarf, she was also much taller and Daridar hit her below her center of gravity. The two went down in a spinning fall, with Daridar landing on top of Besaline. Daridar reacted far faster than the heavy slave master, and her hand closed around Besaline's throat, her fingers digging into the excess fat, closing on Besaline's windpipe, with a strength that scared the slave master. Daridar's well nailed fingers, of the other hand, came close to her eyes. "Not a sound," Daridar hissed. Besaline, not the bravest of people without support of her master, quickly lay very still, her frightened eyes looking into the raging eyes of the dwarf. "Where are we?" Daridar hissed again. "Who are you?" she added quickly, for she had seen the small amulet around the woman's neck.

"I am Besaline, keeper of the female slaves," she whispered her trembling answer. "We are near the rear gate of the castle," she added carefully. "How did you get out of the cell?" she asked in surprise, for Besaline had been in the back of the room when Daridar had been dropped in front of Brandaro. Daridar's eyes took on a intense look that frightened the slave master even more.

"Males think with only one purpose," she whispered, her face getting closer to Besaline's. "When you defeat that, they are nothing." A small, very frightening grin, came to Daridar's lips. Besaline could only look into the eyes of the dwarf as an answer. "Do you know where the female slave called Isabella is?" Daridar asked. Besaline stared into the dwarfs eyes, and tried to shake her head, slowly. "The one Brandaro seeks," Daridar added. Besaline's eyes opened wider.

"How do you know of her?" Besaline whispered. Daridar's face came even closer.

"She has powers, and has made contact with those she was taken from. She is helping them to launch an attack against Brandaro, and to be freed by them," Daridar whispered back. "If you want to be saved from the rule of Brandaro, and be free when he is defeated, you will help me. Otherwise, I will kill you now." Daridar's nails drew closer to Besaline's eyes, and her hand tightened on the slave master throat. Daridar was very surprised when Besaline began to grow a smile.

"What can I do to help with the defeat of Brandaro?" Besaline asked, as her smile continued to grow.

<hr />

As the races from the Realm and Ventoria donned their amulets, and were informing the new arrivals of all they had discovered of Neponia, a cart arrived. Power Stones were handed out to any that possessed magical power. The fairy folk and imps were too small to wear one, but it had already been decided that with their speed, and the wearing of the Milky Quartz made for their size, as well as the Amplifying stones left from the battle with the Dark Domain, that they would be safe without the power stones. Michele called for the races leaders, the Ventorian leader, and Neponities, to gather, and she would explain what her father, mother, and siblings, had decided the best course of actions for the defenses. She started by explaining that it was thought that there should be spotters, fairy folk and imps, stationed in all areas around Capital City, with a few of the more magically powerful ones with them. When the attackers appeared, the defending forces could be told quickly, and converge on that area. The larger, faster ones, making sure the slower were brought as well. They had begun to establish areas for the spotters when Cartope, Nepopea, and Seastaria, charged into the clearing.

"The attackers are coming," Cartope announced to all. "Seastaria has seen that they come soon," she added, and looks were exchanged among those of the Realm, Ventoria, and Neponia. Barsynia told Somora what she had heard.

Isabella and Kris were delicately making their way through the tunnel as they listened to the muffled voices of Morselia and Caratelia. They froze when the roaring voice of Brandaro came clearly through the wall. "Prepare my armor, we attack now!" he roared, and Kris and Isabella shared worried looks, in the dim light of the tunnel. The excited voices of the two women and the sounds of rattling armor easily covered Isabella's whisper as she told Penelopy of what was happening. Kris pulled her on through the tunnel, finally stopping at a wall that blocked their way.

"What do we do now?" Isabella quietly asked. Kris held her finger to her lips and placed her ear to the wall. She listened for at least two minutes, and then nodded to Isabella. She pressed several places on the wall and one of the large bottom stones swung inward. Kris released Isabella's hand and crawled through the opening, with Isabella right behind her. After they stood, they turned back to the wall they had just come through, and Kris pressed several more places and the stone swung closed.

Kris smiled at Isabella, as they both turned around, and looked into very surprised faces of Daridar and Besaline.

"Isabella," Kris said softly, extending her hand towards the dwarf; "may I present Daridar. Besaline I believe you already know." Daridar and Besaline looked back and forth between Kris and Isabella, while Isabella looked back and forth between Daridar, and the slave master.

"I thought you were in the cell," Isabella said to Daridar.

"*You're*, the one Brandaro's been looking for?" Daridar pointed at Isabella as she looked the girl up and down. Daridar's question had a ridiculing emphases on the word "You're".

"You're the one the slaves have been rumoring of?" Besaline asked quietly, as she pointed at Kris. Kris bowed with a very wide grin.

"I am here to get you out of here," Daridar told Isabella, her fists on her hips, and a look of strength. Isabella stared at the dwarf as her brows lifted slowly. She then shook her head and looked to Besaline.

"Get these things off of me," she ordered, holding out her wrists and lifting her head slightly. Besaline nodded and muttered as she moved her hands. The necklace and bracelets fell to the floor. Isabella immediately tried to call to Namson. There was no response. She looked to Kris and there was worry in her eyes. "They can't hear me," she said softly.

"Well I could!" Daridar said through gritted teeth, rubbing her head.

"Brandaro keeps a shielding on the castle, so none can attack him," Besaline said meekly. "And, the devices you wore have a lingering effect." Isabella looked at her and then to Kris. She held out her hand and Kris took it.

"Penelopy, if you can hear me, tell the Overseer I must talk to him immediately." Tarressa'a voice came to her.

"He's right here, what do you need?" Penelope's question came to her.

"Tell him that there is a shielding around the castle! I've gotten the shielding devises off me, but have been told that there is a lingering effect, and I'm not sure how much of my powers I have use of."

"Are you someplace safe?" Tarressa's voice asked Namson's question. Isabella looked to Kris.

"We need a place of safety, now." Kris looked around and then smiled at her.

"Come on, I know just the place, and it's close," she said, leading Isabella off. Daridar and Besaline looked to each other, and then to the two walking away.

"Wait for us," Daridar said as she and Besaline followed. "I'm supposed to be saving you!"

The four guards who had been ordered to take Porkligor and Rentaring to the inquisitors, never saw the attack coming. Brandaro had ordered the two Captains to be interrogated, and they did not suspect that the two Captains may not have agreed with their fate. "Take da two's on ya's side." Porkligor whispered as they turned the corner of the hallway. "Now!" They hadn't even been tied, all thinking that the roughing up they had received from Telposar and Belidaria would keep them docile. Rentaring slammed the heads of the two guards on his side, into the wall with a strength no one would have thought the skinny man possessed. Porkligor simply clanged the heads of the two on his side, together. The two stood looking at the fallen and unconscious guards.

"Wha now?" Rentaring asked, his adrenalin causing him to pant slightly. Porkligor chuckled as he turned to his coconspirator.

"Brandaro go'n tack soon," Porkligor told Rentaring. "We gader ours men's and be's ready whe he comes back, dat wha! Come on!" Porkligor grabbed Rentaring's arm and led him off to another exit from the castle, that not many knew of.

───※─────

Namson kept glancing at Penelopy as they waited for Isabella to find a safe hiding place. Glornina, Zachia, Emma, and Glorian, sat on the couch, and watched the not so patient pacing of the Overseer. Calteen and Salear came through their special door in the wall, and they were followed by twelve of the biggest faxlies they could find, as well as eight well muscled imps. They all landed on the desk, and Namson looked at Calteen with surprise, about the imps.

"They volunteered," the leader of the Realm fairy folk said simply, with a small shrug. Namson grinned and nodded, with a slight bow to the imps. The imps returned the bow with wide grins of their own.

"Namson?" Glornina asked quietly. "Are you planning on sending them first?" Her question was no louder than her first word. Namson turned to her and nodded, then glanced at Penelopy. The girl tried to smile an apology, and shook her head.

⁓⁓•◦※◦●※◉※●◦※◦•⁓⁓

"There is nothing but storage rooms down here," Besaline said as they stepped from the third stair case they had descended, and moved down the hall.

"Exactly," Kris said in response. After about three hundred feet, Kris stopped in front of a wall, quickly touched four different places, and a door about five feet tall and two feet wide, swung open. "Come on," Kris told all, and pulled Isabella into the room. They entered a room that was at least thirty feet square. There was a bed, a small stove, and several boxes stacked in one corner. "Emergency quarters," Kris told Isabella. "This is about as safe as it can get. Call your people." Isabella nodded and talked to Penelopy.

"She's ready Overseer," Penelopy said with a grin. Namson nodded and looked to Tarressa.

"Concentrate on her, but do not talk yet," he told her. She nodded and again closed her eyes. Namson went to the desk and opened the top left drawer. He took out a Milky Quartz amulet and the Power Stone he had gotten from Neponia. He went to Tarressa and placed his hand on her shoulder. "Tell her I am going to try and spell a Milk Stone, and a Power Stone to her, and I need to know if she gets them, intact." Terressa nodded and sent Namson's words.

"She understands," Penelopy said, looking to what he held. Namson stared at the two amulets he held and they suddenly disappeared. "She has them," Penelopy almost screamed. Namson looked to her and his smile grew. With his hand still on Terressa'a shoulders he looked to those on the desk.

"As close together as you can get," he told them. Calteen and Salear moved from the rest as they huddle together. "I have to use a very tight beam to penetrate the shielding. Alright Tarressa, tell her I'm sending her some flying help." Tarressa nodded and transmitted his words.

"She understands," Penelopy stated with a smile. Namson stared at the faxlies and imps, and they suddenly disappeared. "They have arrived and are scaring the hell out of all that are with her," Penelopy said. "She is explaining to the others who the fairy folk, and imps, are." Namson again nodded.

"Tarressa, tell her that the faxlies will tell her of my plans, and she is to do all she can to help them." Terressa again nodded with her eyes still closed, and passed on Namson's instructions.

"She says she understands, but has to break connection to do more. She will talk again when they have a final plan," Penelopy said, and then whispered more. "I love you too honey, please be careful." Tarressa dutifully sent her words. Namson turned to his wife and children.

"Zachia, contact the other domains and start gathering as many as you can for our assault on Bandarson." His son nodded and he, Emma, and Glorian, disappeared. Glornina rose and came to him.

"Can you open a portal into the castle?" she asked softly. Namson shook his head.

"No, the shielding is too strong, but with the information the fairies and imps, can send us, I can anywhere else, and the rest we should be able to deal with." Glornina looked at him in confusion. He smiled at her. "The shielding of the castle is a magical block, not a physical one," he said softly, and smiled with his wife, as she understood.

<hr />

Neponities, Cartope, and Michele, and the women's mates, watched from a small rise, just southeast of the city, as the defense forces spread out around that part of the Capital City, for that was where Seastaria had said the bandits would attack. "I have just been told that the next load of Milky Quartz amulets are ready to be sent," Michele said, and another crate appeared in the clearing. Neponities looked to Traredonar.

"Pass those out to all you can, quickly," she told him. He bowed, grabbed the box, and took it towards the City.

"It's the waiting I hate," Cartope muttered as she watched the three dragons that circled above the city.

"We better get to the city ourselves," Michele stated. Neponities nodded and led the them towards the city that had been her home her entire life. She hoped that it would be for her future. The sun was just beginning its caress of the horizon.

<hr />

Brandaro looked over the troops he had gathered in the large court yard of his castle. He smiled at them, and they smiled back. "We go," he commanded and a portal opened. He led the way into it. Telposar and Belidaria followed him, and the troops followed them.

<hr />

Isabella found out quickly that she and Daridar could talk with many of the faxlies and imps. She also discovered that most of her magical talents had returned, and she was stronger than she had ever been, because there was now anger to enhance her powers. When they had finally worked out their plan, with an surprising amount of help from Besaline, on the design of the castles interior, she touched Kris's hand and told Penelopy, and so Namson, what they were about. After that, Kris opened the door of the chamber, and the imps and faxlies flew out, each with their own jobs to do.

Namson watched as his troops gathered from the Realm as well as all the other domains. It had only taken several hours to gather them. Namson looked to the sun, almost gone.

Porkligor and Rentaring had gathered their own troops, and began sneaking them into the castle. Porkligor had his own agenda, and his first two targets were two women named Morselia and Caratelia.

Mastone couldn't believe how fast he, and the guards with him had gotten lost in all the different tunnels they had found. It would be days before they would finally find their way out.

Brandaro led his troops from the portal, just a few hundred yards from the city's beginning. The sun began to dip below the horizon. He quickly raised his arm, signaling the charge. The entire army had just reached their full charge, yelling as loud as they could, and throwing blast spells, when there came a great roar from the sky above them. Still in a full charge, they all looked up. What they saw caused most to come to sliding stop. This of course, caused those behind them to run into them, for all were looking at the three huge winged beasts that were diving at them. Brandaro sent his blast spell at the leading beast as Telposar and Belidaria sent theirs at the other two. The three were stunned that their spells had absolutely no effect on the diving creatures. Then, without any belief by the bandits, huge streams of flames shot from the mouths of the three creatures, towards Brandaro's forces. The screams of the attacking army couldn't cover the roaring of the great hairy beasts that charged from the City, spreading out as they came. They were followed by other huge creatures, and then smaller ones, all sending blast spells at Brandaro, and his forces. The surprised, and now terrified raiders scattered, heading for the forests that flanked both sides of the road they were on. Without warning, more of the beasts came from the trees, as more of the winged beasts came in over the trees and flamed them back towards each other. In less than three minutes, the entire band of over a hundred raiders were captured, including Brandaro, Telposar, and Belidaria. They huddled, as dragons, ogres, Ventorians, trolls, and Neponian's, surrounded them.

⌒⌒⋙⋘⋙⋘⋙⋘⋘⋙⋘⋘⋙⋘⋙⋘

Porkligor and Rentaring quickly began to implement their plan, to be in control of the castle when Brandaro returned. They started taking out the guards still at the castle. Rentaring's half of the forces took the troops that were the outer circle, which included the guards at gates and wall turrets, as well as the guards that patrolled the court yard, and the rooms and halls near the outer walls. Porkligor headed his troops into the interior of the castle. He quickly advanced on the private quarters of Brandaro's women.

Fairy folk began reporting back to Isabella, including the surprise attacks of Porkligor and Rentaring. Isabella told Penelopy, and then it came to Namson. He began to smile as he realized what those attacks meant. He prepared his troops quickly. With Zachia leading one division, he another, Glornina the third, and Tarson, the fourth, he opened four portals, and the forces of the Realm entered the Bandarson Domain. Namson was not surprised to see Melsikan and Carl beside him as he led his division into the portal. No one seemed to notice the six extra that followed each of Glornina's and Tarson's troops.

Brandaro was very close to Telposar and Belidaria. He leaned to them as he watched the surrounding defenders. "Watch me, and do as I do," he whispered, and they gave slight nods of understanding. The three started to ease their way to the outer fringe of the huddled bandits. Brandaro watched as the defenders moved about. He waited until there were three of the shorter ones near, and no others. He suddenly burst into a run, snatching the Milk Stone from the neck of one of the trolls, and ran on. Telposar and Belidaria were right behind him, snatching the stones from the necks of other two trolls. The three had so surprised the defenders with their escape, that the three made the edge of town before anyone started after them. They disappeared into the alley ways of the city, as yells of pursuit were heard, and the setting sun disappeared completely below the horizon.

⚊⚊⚊⚊⚊

Glornina's and Tarson's portals opened on opposite sides of Bandarson City. They and their forces, quickly spread out and advanced on the unsuspecting people of Bandarson. Namson's portal opened in front of the main gate, as Zachia's opened at the rear gate. Dragons were the last to come from the portals and quickly took to the air. Namson and Melsikan, the first to come from their portal, and Zachia, with Tarson's son Praton beside him, being the first from their portal, began hurling blast spells as soon as they exited the portals. This eliminated the guards at the gates, and the gates, immediately. The ones very quickly coming behind them, aimed at the troops on the walls above the gates. Namson and Melsikan, Zachia and Praton, charged through the destroyed gates with their divisions right behind them. The forces of Rentaring suddenly had two problems. The first was the guards they had captured, and the caging of them. The second being the unexpected, onrushing forces. They had no idea who these newcomers were, or where they had come from. Most of Rentaring's forces decided that this was not a good place to be, and threw down their weapons and tried to flee. With the accurate description of the castle they had been given, wolves and trolls were quickly able to cut off their escape, and most all were captured, and added the castle guards already caged. Porkligor, unaware of the events happening in the other parts of the castle, crashed into Brandaro's bedroom and found Morselia and Caratelia on the large bed, involved in a very active session with quite a few slaves, both male and female.

"What do you think you are doing?" Morselia screamed at him as eight soldiers followed him into the room. The men were leering and grinning as Morselia came off the bed and faced them, completely naked.

"Get'n me's due!" Porkligor said as he looked the women up and down. "I's gets ya both first and den me's men's get ya!" He started to advance, and his troops followed him. The slaves all cringed at the head of the bed, but Morselia and Caratelia, who had come off the bed and now stood beside Morselia, faced the assault, and there was rage in their eyes.

"You aren't that lucky!" Morselia roared at the fat Captain as she and Caratelia charged Porkligor, and the men with him. Neither the fat Captain, nor his troops, were prepared for the deadly ferocity the two very powerful women were capable of, and they went down screaming, without any more than a lucky grope at best. Porkligor had never considered the fact that in order to be Brandaro's women, Morselia and Caratelia had to be tough enough to be able to take care of themselves.

Brandaro, Telposar, and Belidaria ran through the alleys of Capital City, looking for some place of safety. They stayed to the shadows, and were forced to hide often, as the dragons, Eagles, and bats, searched from the air. The much smaller fairy folk and imps, flying just high enough they couldn't be reached, also hunted them. The three were completely frustrated that when they would try to hit them with a spell, it had no effect. They seemed to be everywhere, and constantly told the defense forces of their whereabouts.

"Brandaro, we cannot run forever," Belidaria whispered between her pants. They were hiding behind some large boxes. They had all donned the amulets they had taken from the trolls, and knew that they were safe from the blast spells sent at them, but they knew they could not fight, hand to hand, with the many large beasts, and humans, that chased them.

"I know that," Brandaro growled at her. "We have got to find a place we can battle them. A place where we have a possibility of defending ourselves. I want to hurt them, to make them bow to me, to kill those who would think to defy me!" he hissed, and the other two exchanged doubtful glances.

"Brandaro," Telposar said. "We have no weapons, but the daggers we carry. Our spells have no affect! How are we to battle them?" Brandaro spun, and looked into his henchman's eyes. Rage flared from his eyes.

"We can conjure spears, and bows, arrows, even rocks," he spit at Telposar. Telposar felt fear from Brandaro's look, and voice. He quickly nodded as the voices of several of the fairy folk came to them.

"They are here!" the voices cried out, and several of the dragons homed in on the three, one of which called to Michele, and told her where the fugitives were hiding. The sound of closing ogres, Ventorians, and trolls, came to their ears.

"Damn those little monsters!" Brandaro cried out and, led the three in a direction he thought he could find the defensive point he sought.

Glornina led her forces into the west side of the city as Tarson came from the east. The fairy folk that Namson had sent, had given a very accurate description of the cities layout and the two forces drove the people towards the huge square, in the center of the city. With the dragons roaring at them, and the eagles and bats, screaming at them, all from the air, plus the never seen before, very big ogres, Ventorians, and Natharian's, threatening them, they quickly complied and with terror, began to gather in the square. Fairy folk and imps would get into the places of hiding that many had sought, and the wolves and trolls would drive them from their refuge. The six, who had followed each of the armies, dropped back from the regular fighters, and the twelve met later, to discuss what they were going to do here in this domain. As the people of Bandarson were being gathered, they would glance to the two humongous statues that sided the wide street that led to the main gate of the castle. One was the statue of Bandaro, the founder of the Bandits Domain, and the other was of

Brandaro, the current ruler. The people wondered why he was not protecting them.

⁓⁕⋄⋆⊙⊙⋆⋄⁕⁓

Brandaro, Telposar, and Belidaria, looked to the amphitheater from the end of the alley. Telposar and Belidaria looked to Brando, and were surprised to see him smiling. "From here we will teach these fools the true power that is Bandarson!" Brandaro said much too loudly. "Come," he ordered and led them as they sprinted across the hundred and fifty yards of open area, to the center of the three openings in the wall that surrounded the amphitheater. "We have got them now," Brandaro growled, a look of hatred and pleasure, coming to his eyes. "Go to the other openings and begin to send everything you can at them," Brandaro ordered between gasps for breath. The other two nodded. Telposar went right as Belidaria went left. They quickly began sending everything they could conjure at the advancing forces. Michele saw the danger of what the three were going to do, and simply placed a blocking spell, thirty feet out from the wall. The would be missiles of death, that the bandits sent, simply hit the barrier, and fell to the ground. Two of the dragons, one from one side, and one from the opposite, flamed the top of the wall, driving the three back from it and down the hill to the stage of the amphitheater. There they stood, sure of their victory, as the defense forces came through the openings, and lined up against the inside of the wall. Neponities stepped forward.

"Surrender or die," was all she told them. Brandaro roared as did Telposar to his right and Belidaria to his left. Telposar and Belidaria, each placed one hand on Brandaro's shoulders, giving him their power, and he raised his hands in the air.

"You are to be the ones to die!" he bellowed and began his incantation.

"Everybody, outside of the wall," Michele screamed, both in thought, and voice, for she had heard the warning from Wenzorn. She understood the danger, of what would happen, if someone with power tried to use the maximum effect of the stones. All of the defenders of Neponia, scrambled out of the amphitheater, by way the three openings. Brandaro laughed loudly.

"You cannot run from me now," he screamed, now sure of their victory, because of the running of their victims. A bat, who was still in the air, unfortunately was caught in the resulting blast, but lived to tell what happened next.

"The three medallions they wore, became bright lights," the bat started his telling. "Suddenly, lightning flashed between the medallions, and the three of them were encompassed in a great ball of light, then it exploded."

As the explosion had spread out in a circle, the back half of the circle was reflected off the stone walls of the amphitheater, behind the three, and added a second wave to the destructive effect of the shock waves. It was said later that they were all very lucky that only six Neponian's had died from the destruction of wall, and part of the city beyond, but there were hundreds of wounded, many severely, including many of those of the Realm and Ventoria. Nothing of the three bandits was ever found. All knew that the three had been consumed by the explosion. It took years to completely remove the scorching of stage and theaters walls.

———

"We have not found her anywhere," Melsikan told Namson, as Zachia and Praton joined them. Namson smiled at him.

"Talk to her," he said.

"I thought there is a shielding," Melsikan said with furrowed brows. Namson shook his head with a smile.

"Not on the inside. Go ahead, call to her," Namson said, as an imp flew to them.

"Are you Melsikan?" the imp asked, looking to the young man. Melsikan nodded. "I know where Isabella is, come with me." The imp said, and flew off. Melsikan and Carl were right behind him.

———

Namson continued to smile as he watched the two run off and then he turned to his oldest son. "Come on, we're not done yet," he said. Zachia nodded and followed him as he headed for the center of the castle, where they knew Brandaro's private quarters were. They entered the throne room and looked around at the empty room.

"Where is everybody?" Zachia asked in almost a whisper. Namson shrugged and started for the hallway that he had been told, led to Brandaro's private quarters. He was only slightly surprised when he opened the door and saw the two large women trying to comfort those on the bed, and the bodies of Porkligor and his soldiers, lying about. All had managed to find gowns to put on and Morselia and Caratelia turned to face the two who had entered.

"What do you want here?" Caratelia asked in an angry voice. "Get out!"

"This is the Overseer of the Realm! The rule of this Domain is defeated," Zachia told them. Their faces turned angry and started for Namson and Zachia. They were both very surprised that with no hand movement seen, or sound of voice, they were abruptly locked in a immobilization spell. Namson smiled at them with only his lips.

"You heard my son," he told them, his anger clear in his voice. "Brandaro is no longer in power here, and neither are you two!" he told them. "The cruelties that Brandaro wielded, can no longer hurt the peoples of this domain!"

Melsikan was quickly ahead of Carl, as they chased the imp, but the shorter Carl never got that far behind. As they stepped from the bottom step of the third flight of stairs, they saw the wall ahead, swing inward, and Isabella came out, in a run. She was followed by Kris. Melsikan took her into his arms, and his lips met hers with desperation. Carl started to turn from the painful sight, his hands shoved deeply into his pockets. As he turned, his eyes met those of Kris. His mouth fell open, almost as far as his eyes did, and Kris giggled.

"Oh Melsikan," Isabella whispered as their kiss ended, and the powerful embrace began. "I so feared I would never see you again." Her tears trying to hide her words.

"No way my love," he whispered to her, his tears deepening his voice. "You cannot get away from me by being simply kidnapped." Even through her tears, all heard her sigh.

Chapter Eight

Healers from all the domains, came to Neponia. Carpenters, stonemason, merchants, and those who would be part of the labor force, flooded Neponia, to aid with the rebuilding of the City. There were also some who came, did so with a different purpose.

Namson and most of the invading armies, stayed on Bandarson, and sorted out who was to be punished, and for what. They also acted as a security force, until a trusted police force of Bandarsonite's could be formed. It took a week and a half, but Namson was finally able to assign the role of Director to one, and approved the choices made for those who would be of his cabinet. One of those choices was a female dwarf named Daridar, whose primary job was to report on the happenings in Bandarson, to the Realm. Melsikan, Isabella, Carl, and Kris, had returned to the Realm immediately, where they picked up Terressa, Penelopy, and Marcus, and then went on to Zentler.

The horrible part of Isabella's return, was having to tell the loved ones of the other eight girls, who had been taken with her, that none had survived, though she did not tell them what abuse they had suffered. Father's tried stoically not to weep, as they held their sobbing wives. Most did not succeed.

One of the surprising things that came from all that had happened, was that Terressa had lost almost all of her clumsiness! Not all, but most. The entire town of Zentler was amazed, and pleased.

The entire town threw a party in honor of Isabella's safe return. During that party, Isabella and Melsikan were married. It was also during that party that Gordon and Xanaporia got the biggest of surprises.

It would seem that many who lived in Zentler during the time of Willy's term as Mayor, had suspected many of the happenings in, and around the town. They in turn had told their children, who witnessed many things of their own. A selected committee told their current Mayor and his wife, that they knew of, and accepted, the magical talents that at least an eighth of the population possessed! They told the Mayor, and his wife, that they had no intention of letting anyone that was not of Zentler, to know about it. *We'll just keep it our little secret*, was the common phrase used. The town of Zentler's rebuilding went much faster from then on. Dolores

Remmy sent a request to Somora, for a male to woo Terressa.

Somora had listened as his seers and talkers, who had hidden their powers from Castope, as they told him of the events as they unfolded. His smile stayed constant during all of the telling. "When do we attack?" Perilia asked. Somora turned to her and saw the blood lust in her eyes. He slowly shook his head, and Perilia looked angry. Somora looked to his gathered followers, who had followed him through the tunnel in the southern mountains, from the Dark City. His smile grew wider.

"First, we will slowly work our way into the groups that have the power, and then we will begin to break that control!" His voice getting louder with each word. "As we gain more, and more, of the positions that will allow us to maneuver those of power, we will infiltrate the other domains and penetrate their power as well."

"Why the city of Zentler?" Dospora asked. "It isn't a magical place, and there is no power there." Somora smiled at her.

"This Isabella, is from Zentler, as is the male she wed. They are both, very powerful magical talents, and, there are many who have a major role in the lives of those in the Realm," he told her and all gathered. "It will be the back door we shall use to further penetrate the Realm!" The crowd around him cheered for their coming victory.

────

Gordon and Xanaporia had taken Kris into their home. Gordon was not surprised when Carl showed up at his door, the morning after the party.

"Good morning Carl," Gordon said as a small grin grew on his lips. "To what do we owe this visit?" Carl blushed and Gordon heard a hushed giggle behind him.

"Is Kris here?" Carl asked quietly, only glancing at Gordon. Kris came around Gordon, cutting off anything Gordon might have said.

"Good morning Carl," she said coyly, smiling. Xanaporia, who had walked from the kitchen with Kris, pulled Gordon from the doorway, and led him back to the kitchen table. Carl swallowed hard, and his blush became more pronounced.

"I was wondering if maybe, you know, if you want to that is, would you, ah, take a walk with me?" He had tried to be suave, but it just wasn't to be. Kris took his arm as she pulled the door closed behind her.

"I'd like that," she told him. "Maybe you could show me around the town?" she suggested. Carl grinned, still blushing.

"Sure," he told her nodding. Carl again showing his worldliness. Kris laughed as they walked from the house. From then on, they were seen together constantly, and it did not take very much effort, on anyone's part, to see the love that was being found by both. A month later they were wed, and with the combined efforts of Carl, Kris, Melsikan, Isabella, Marcus, and Penelopy, the three couples, and a quite few from the town, built three houses, not too far from each other, on the south west edge of town. Shortly after they were all able to move into their homes, they, and most of the town of Zentler, were surprised to see Terressa in the company of a man who had only arrived in town a week after their return, and he seemed quite interested in her. They maybe should have questioned him?

Namson and Glornina traveled to Neponia, after leaving Bandarson, leaving Zachia and Emma, who had joined him there, to finish up the minor details. The Overseer and Mistress of the Realm, were impressed with the progress of the rebuilding of Capital City, as well as the recoveries of the injured. They were also very proud of their youngest daughters efforts, for the defense of Neponia, and the aid in the recoveries of the wounded. Neponities and Cartope led them, Michele and Crendoran, on a tour of the infirmary and the city.

"With the generous and timely assistance of those from domains we had no idea even existed, Neponia is recovering quickly, and we owe it all to you Overseer," Neponities said. Namson smiled, slowly shaking his head.

"I think you owe nothing Neponities," he told her gently. "My only hope is that you, and all of Neponia, would join in the alliance of all peaceful Magical Domains. For when we all work together, there is very little that cannot be accomplished." Neponities nodded and looked to Namson.

"It was our hope that we would be asked," she told him. "The Queen of the Northern Section, Nepelia, has already committed to that end, but the Queen of the Southern Section, Nepolia, has reservations. My daughter, Nepanities, and Cartope, are going there as soon as we have brought the city to it proper self again, to try and convince them of the value of joining with the Realm." Namson and Glornina nodded their agreement, but then Namson frowned slightly.

"What reservations does she have?" he asked the Queen of the Central Section. She stopped and looked to the Overseer.

"Nepolia has always had the tendency of greed," she told him, her voice turning to a hardness. "We have many times, had to remind her of the borders that she continually tries to move in her favor." Namson lifted one brow slightly.

"Neponities and I have formed an idea that we feel will bring her to understand the value of the joining the Domains of Rightful Magic" Cartope said with a small smile, but her eyes spoke differently.

"Papa, even since I've been here, there has been two happenings of border disputes," Michele said quietly.

"Do not worry Overseer," Neponities said quickly. "We can handle Nepolia, and I'm sure that she will see the truth, and value, of joining." Namson glanced to Michele and saw concern in her eyes. He turned to Neponities.

"I will leave this matter with Your Majesty, but please remember, that you only need to call, and we will come," he told her and there was a tone in his voice she did not miss.

"Thank you Overseer. I will not forget," Neponities stated as she bowed. Namson and Glornina returned her bow.

"Papa, Crendoran and I are going to stay until all have recovered from their wounds," Michele said. Glornina put her arm around her daughter, and smiled at her.

"We would have been surprised if you had not," she told Michele, who blushed slightly and leaned closer to her mother, whispering to her. Glornina's eyes flew open, and then she hugged Michele. Namson looked at the two, and smiled.

"You're pregnant, again?" he asked in a sigh. Michele nodded, her blush deepening. Namson held his smile as he slowly shook his head. "Don't you know what causes that yet?" Michele nodded rapidly, and her blush increased, as did her smile. That got them all laughing as Namson gave his daughter a hug. When they finally separated, they all started back to the Queens palace, which surprisingly, was not much bigger than most of the houses in the city. One hour later, Namson opened a portal and he, Glornina, and any of the mending who were ambulatory enough, returned to the Realm.

CHAPTER NINE

Cenlinas watched her biological twins, the results of her short time as a young Brandaro's bed slave, as they played, if any could say the battle they fought, was play. The twins, now near full grown, which was far larger than most their ages, fought as many would fear fighting. There was no concession to failure. There was no lessening of intent, or desire to win. Even though the boy was much stronger, the girl was more cunning. Both bled from wounds, but each attack, each assault, each lunge, was met with a parry, and returned damage. They would circle. They would never take their eyes from the other. They both smiled as they fought. Each time a wound was inflicted, a cry of success was issued by the one causing it. But, it was quickly answered with a cry of success, as the other inflicted a wound. Neither seemed to have an advantage, Neither could claim victory. At best, it was a bloody, and painful, draw.

Cenlinas's anger boiled within her. Their father had been the most powerful of rulers. Their father had brought Bandarson to its highest. His murder, made her son, the son of Brandaro, Bandarson's new ruler! She almost smiled as she neared them, to tell them of their fathers murder. How those of the Realm, had turned the peoples of Bandarson, against the memory of their father. How the Realm, had lied of their fathers prowess, and had lied about the extent of pain and suffering, he had caused them, before his death!

She had spent many years telling of the greatness of the one she had been a bed slave to. She would now spend her time, telling of the wrongs done against Brandaro and those of Bandarson. She would spend many more years, teaching her children to hate the Realm, and the Overseer, for his distortion of the greatness made by the one she would always love, Brandaro! Within a year of Brandaro's death, in Bandarson City, an election was held, and the final insult to Brandaro's memory was made. They had elected the dwarf, Daridar, as Mayor. They had placed the control of all Bandarson, the entire domain, in the hands of a Dwarf! It was then, that others' started to listen to Cenlinas, and there were many that agreed with her!

—∿∙⚬⊛⚬⊛⚬∙∿—

In the following year, the young couples of Zentler, and all of the magical domains, became parents. Those who had been injured on Neponia, healed, and thrived. The Queen of the Southern Section, submitted to the will of the other two Queens, but there was resentment. Namson and Glornina, and all of those of the Realm, settled into the daily lives of happiness. The citizens of Bandarson changed the name of their Domain to Namsia, but not of those of the outer regions, especially Cenlinas, agreed with the change. Life seemed to come to a state of contentment. But, with all contentment, it cannot last!

CHARACTERS

HUMAN

<u>Aaralyn</u>-magical powers, very high—daughter of Croldena and Meladiana—younger sister of Creldora—wife of Jarponer

<u>Ava</u>—magical power, unknown latent, high—mistress of Gordon when he first becomes mayor of Zentler—mother of Isabella

<u>Baldor</u>—magical powers, high—(Dremlor)—Somora's spy to the Realm

<u>Barrett</u>—magical powers, high—son of Edward and Carla—older brother of Karrie—husband of Quentia—father of Barator and Qualaren

<u>Barsynia</u>—magical powers, high—Somora's spy to Neponia(came with Cartope's group)-

Barttel—magical powers, high—son of Gordon and Xanaporia—older brother of Xanaleria- husband of Alexania

Belkor—magical powers, very high—grandson of Mentalon, Xanadera, Namson, Glornina—son of Braxton and Glorian—younger brother of Heather—twin brother of Telkor

Braxton—magical powers, med(powerful sensor)—son of Mentalon and Xanadera—younger brother of Alexania—husband of Glorian—father of Heather, Telkor, Belkor-(Canyon)

Carl Bries—no magical powers—older brother of Terressa—husband of Kris

Carla—magical powers, high, talker and seer-wife of Edward—mother of Barrett and Karrie- grandmother of Barator, Qualaren, Norsalon, Kamernia

Creldora—magical powers, high—son of Croldena and Meladiana—older brother of Aaralyn

Crendoran—magical powers, high—son of Vandora and Gerpinos—younger brother of Nimranson and Helinos—husband of Michele

Croldena—Corsendorian general—magical powers, med—husband of Meladiana—father of Creldora and Aaralyn—grandfather of Xanarensia, Cranepena, Crenorett, Velsimor

Dafnorian—magical powers, very, very high—granddaughter of Vandora, Gerpinos, Namson, Glornina—daughter of Crendoran and Michele—younger sister of Mearlanor—older sister of Ramnarson—wife of Prelimor

Dolores Remmy—magical powers, high(Dremlor)—Somora's spy in Zentler—Gordon's secretary

Dospora—magical powers, high(Dremlor)-second comate of Somora—escapee from the Dark City of Castope

Edward—Magical power, high—Keeper, N.W. Domain—husband of Carla—father of Barrett and Karrie-grandfather of Barator, Qualaren, Kriston, Norsalon, Kamernia

Emma—magical powers, high—daughter of Darren and Meligan—older sister of Cartland—wife of Zachia—mother of Mike, Mergania, Minsitoria

Giorgio Sordian—magical powers, latent, very high—son of Penelopy and Marcus—older brother of Isabella(Bella)

Glorian—magical powers, very, very high—daughter of Namson and Glornina—younger sister of Zachia—older sister of Michele—wife of Braxton—mother of Heather, Telkor, Belkor(Plain)

Glornina—magical powers, very, very high—wife of Namson—mother of Zachia, Glorian,

Michele—grandmother of Mike, Mergania, Minsitoria, Heather, Telkor, Belkor, Mearlanor, Dafnorian, Ramnarson

Gordon—magical powers, med—mayor of Zentler—husband of Xanaporia—father of Isabella, Barttel and Xanaleria—grandfather of Alexia, Sartoran, Mertilan, Xanapordia

Isabella—magical powers, very, very high—illegitimate daughter of Gordon and Ava—cousin of Penelopy Barns, by mothers side—aids in the overthrow of Bandarson—kidnapped and held as Brandaro's personal slave—becomes wife of Melsikan

Jarponer—magical powers, very high—son of Jarsalon and Quentoria—younger brother of Quentia- husband of Aaralyn

Jarsolan—magical powers, high—husband of Quentoria—father of Quentia and Jarponer

Karrie—magical powers, very high—daughter of Edward and Carla—younger sister of Barrett-wife of Narmon—mother of Norsalon and Kamernia

Kris—magical powers, low—orphan on Bandarson—hides Isabella from Brandaro—helps channel Isabella to contact Penelopy—wife of Carl—mother of Nathan,

Marcus Sordian—no magical powers—son of Giorgio Sordian(old)—husband of Penelopy—father of Giorgio, and Isabella

Mearlanor—magical powers, very, very high—granddaughter of Vandora, Gerpinos, Namson,

Glornina—daughter of Crendoran and Michele—older sister of Dafnorian, Ramnarson

Melsikan—magical powers, very high-husband of Isabella

Michele—magical powers, very, very high—daughter of Namson and Glornina—younger sister of Zachia and Glorian—wife of Crendoran—mother of Mearlanor, Dafnorian, Ramnarson(Corsendora)

Namson—magical powers, ultra high—Overseer of the Realm—husband of Glornina—father of Zachia(young), Glorian, Michele—grandfather of Mike, Mergania, Minsitoria, Heather, Telkor, Belkor, Mearlanor, Dafnorian, Ramnarson

Paolaria—magical powers, very high—daughter of Crandon and Pentilian—younger sister of

Jarsona—wife of Karlten—mother of Bartoran and Peliaria

Penelopy Barns(Zentler)—no magical powers(can talk with Isabella, but doesn't know it until

Isabella calls to her)—cousin of Isabella's, on her mother's side—becomes direct link to her—wife of Marcus—mother of Giorgio, Isabella(Bella)

Pentilian—magical powers, very high—wife of Crandon—mother of Jarsona and Paolaria- grandmother of Nariana, Estinaria, Bartoran, Peliaria

Perilia—magical powers, high(sorceress)—first comate of Somora—escapee from the Dark City of Castope

Pete—no magical powers—bartender in Zentler

Prelilian—magical powers, very high—wife of Tarson—mother of Praton and Narmon-

Quansloe—magical powers, very high—Keeper of the Plain—son of Marie and Quensloe—younger brother of Jardan, Narisha—twin brother of Drayson—husband of Hannah—father of Polly and Selista—grandfather of Micky, Meligan, Edgar, Prelilian—great grandfather of Danaliana, Karlten, Emma, Cartland, Niana, Alana, Praton, Narmon

Quentia—magical powers, very high(seer)—daughter of Jarsolan and Quentoria—older sister of Jarponer—wife of Barrett—mother of Barator and Qualaren

Quentoria—magical powers, high—wife of Jarsolan—mother of Quentia and Jarponer

Somora—magical powers, very high(Dremlor)—King of those who escaped Dark City of Castope

Tarson—magical powers, high—husband of Prelilian—father of Praton and Narmon—grandfather of Pertannor, Magelisa, Norsalon, Kamernia

Terressa Bries—magical powers, powerful talker—younger sister of Carl-wife of Ben

Vandora—Calisonnos Keeper—magical powers, very high—husband of Gerpinos—father of Nimranson, Helinos, Crendoran

Welainia—magical powers, med—nanny for Karrie and Narmon

Xanaleria—magical powers, very high—daughter of Gordon and Xanaporia—younger sister of Barttel—wife of Cartland—mother of Mertilan and Xanapordia

Xanaporia—magical powers, very high—wife of Gordon—mother of Barttel and Xanaleria

Zachia—magical powers, very, very high—son of Namson and Glornina—older brother of Glorian and Michele—husband of Emma—father of Mike, Mergania, Minsitoria

VENTORIA

Barsantorack—magical power, low—plots to over throw Calsorack as ruler of the Bendine—never works, wants everything free—husband of Simerence—father of Paltarack and Vestirence

Calsorack—magical powers, med—Governor of Bendine Island-grandson of Semirack,

Vertirence—son of Semorator and Saterence—husband of Milserence—father of Megarack and Telinrence

Milserence—magical powers, med—wife of Calsorack—mother of Megarack and Telinrence

Paltarack—magical powers high—son of Barsantorack and Simerence—older brother of Vestirence

Salsakor—magical powers, med—wife of Tremarack—mother of Tramerack and Palserence

Semotor—magical powers, high—general of the Armies of Ventoria—husband of Tererence—father of Mensitor and Drurence

Simerence—magical powers, low—wife of Barsantorack—mother of Paltarack and Vestirence

Tererence—magical powers, high—wife of Semoter—mother of Mensitor and Dryrence

Tremarack—magical powers, med—gets talked into trying to usurp Calsorack as leader of Bendine—husband of Salsakor—father of Zanderack and Tremerence

Vestirence—magical powers, high—daughter of Barsantorack and Simerence—younger sister of Paltarack

NEPONIA

Cartope—magical powers, very high—wife of Ralsanac—mother of Carsanac, Marsanac, Nepopea-grandmother of Carponities, Traremidonar, Belanities, Praretidonar, Seastaria

Draretonar—magical powers, high—Chosen Mate of Nepopea—father of Seastaria

Gorgamins—very large, canine predators that roamed the nights

Mearlies—a race, Elfin like, but much smaller, who can make magical amulets and work the crops and are the healers of Neponia

Nepanities—magical powers, very high—daughter of Neponities and Traredonar—mate of Carsanac—mother of Carponities and Trandorar

Neponities—magical powers, high—Queen of the Center Section of Neponia—mate of Traredonar-mother of Nepanities—grandmother of Carponities, Traremidonar

Nepopea—magical powers, very, very high—daughter of Cartope and Ralsanac—mate of Draretonar—mother of Seastaria

Ralsanac—magical powers. very high—husband of Cartope—father of Carsanac, Marsanac,

Nepopea—grandfather of Carponities, Traremidonar, Belanities, Seastaria

Seastaria—Magical powers, very, very high—Granddaughter of Cartope and Ralsanac—daughter of Nepopea and Draretonar—mate of Bartoran

Traredonar—magical powers, high—Chosen Mate of Neponities—father of Nepanities—grandfather of Carponities and Traremidonar

Waltzorn—magical powers, low—second in command of the Mearlies of the Central Section- husband of Yenlince—father of Walzorn and Yarnlince

Walzorn—magical powers low—son of Waltzorn and Yenlince—older brother of Yarnlince

Wanlizorn—magical powers, low—son of Wenzorn and Yonlince—older brother of Yomlince

Wenzorn—magical powers, low—ruler of the Mearlies of the Central Section—husband of Yonlince—father of Wanlizorn and Yomlince

Yarnlince—magical powers, med—daughter of Waltzorn and Yenlince—younger sister of Walzorn

Yenlince—magical powers, med—wife of Waltzorn—mother of Walzorn and Yarnlince

Yomlince—magical powers, med—daughter of Wenzorn and Yonlince—younger sister of Walzorn

Yonlince—magical powers med—wife of Wenzorn—mother of Walzorn and Yomlince

ELVES

Meritilia—wife and talker of Perolon

Perolon—leader of the Elves on Elandif

Phelilon—ambassador from Elandif to the Realm

Phemlon—leader of the elves in the Realm

Telalon—representative to meet with Mearlies—becomes coordinator to reestablish connection between the two races

OGRES

Grandoa—magical powers, low—mate of Gremble—mother of Manable and Minstoa—grandmother of Meathoa, Grimtal, Morgable—great grandmother of Gramable

Gremble—no magical powers—leader of the ogres of the Realm—mate to Grandoa—father of Manable and Minstoa—grandfather of Morgable, Meathoa, Grimtal—great grandfather of Gramable

DRAGONS

<u>Cartile</u>—magical powers, low—leader of dragons of the Realm—mate of Jastile-father of Semitile- grandfather of Zaclitile

<u>Jastile</u>—magical powers, low—mate of Cartile—mother of Semitile—grandmother of Zaclitile—great grandmother of Gloritile and Palastile

<u>Merlintile</u>—magical powers, very high—son of Crastamor and Crelintile—mate of Semitile—father of Zaclitile

<u>Semitile</u>—magical powers, med—mate of Merlintile—mother of Zaclitile

<u>Welerlintile</u>—magical powers, low—mate of Pratlitile—mother of Preslitile and Demsitile

<u>Zaclitile</u>—magical powers, very high—grandson of Cartile, Jastile, Crastamor, Crelintile—son of Semitile and Merlintile—mate of Maratile

FAIRY FOLK

<u>Bartalear</u>—magical powers, high—mate of Heathlear—father of Quelteen and Roseteen

<u>Belear</u>—magical powers, med—mate of Porlear—mother of Morteen and Charlear—grandmother of Delalear, Branteen, Bendilear, Melsiteen

Calteen—magical powers, high—leader of the fairy folk of the Realm—mate of Salear—father of Miteen and Meglear—grandfather of Pratlear, Darateen, Delalear, Branteen

Charlear—magical powers, med—daughter of Porlear and Belear—mate of Tremliteen—mother of Bendilear and Melsiteen

Meglear—magical powers, high—daughter of Calteen and Salear—mate of Morteen—mother of Delalear and Branteen

Salear—magical powers, med—mate of Calteen—mother of Miteen and Meglear

Tremliteen—magical powers, med—messenger for Namson—son of Calear and Pirteen—mate of Charlear—father of Bendilear and Melsiteen

TROLLS(some have magical powers)(Y—yes N—no)

Bilson-(n)—mate of Zardan

Cailson—(n)—mate of Mursel—mother of Zardan

Censon-(y)—med—mate of Coursel-

Coursel-(y)—med—leader of the young trolls of the Plain—mate of Censon—father of Boursel-

Daison-(n)—mate of Porsel

Heathson-(y)-high—mate of Ponsel

Morsel-(y)—low-leader of the young trolls of the Valley—mate of Quenson

Morson-(n)—mate of Worsel

Mursel-(n)—leader of the Plains troll clan—mate of Cailson

Ponsel-(y)—high-leader of the young trolls of the Realm—mate of Heathson

Porsel-(n)—second in command of trolls in the Realm—mate of Daison

Quenson-(y)—med-mate of Morsel

Worsel-(n)—leader of the Valley troll clan—mate of Morson

Zardan-(n)—leader of the troll clan of the Realm—mate of Bilson

BANDARSON—THE BANDITS DOMAIN

Belidaria—Telposar's woman—almost as big and as mean and as tough as Telposar

Besaline—female slave master for Brandaro

Brandaro—ruler of Bandarson

Caratelia—second woman to Brandaro

Daridar—daughter of Pinsikar and Dormadar

Dormadar—mate of Pinsikar—mother of Daridar

Morselia—first woman of Brandaro pasha—whore

Pestikar—one of Pinsikar's spies—mate to Daridar

Pinsikar—minion of Brandaro—a dwarf

Porkligor—fat bandit Capt.—cohort with Rentaring to overthrow Brandaro—raider of Zentler

Rentaring—very skinny Capt. of a band of bandits—very strong though—great greed for power and wealth—Porkligor's cohort in attempt to overthrow Brandaro

Telposar—henchman for Brandaro—loves to hurt and kill—mate of Belidaria